ZODIAC
A Noir Novel from Romania

Anamaria Ionescu
ZODIAC – A Noir Novel from Romania

Copyright © Anamaria Ionescu
Copyright © TRITONIC 2019 for present edition

All rights reserved, including the right to reproduce fragments of the book.

TRITONIC
　5 Coacăzelor street, Bucharest
　e-mail: editura@tritonic.ro
　www.tritonic.ro

Descrierea CIP a Bibliotecii Naționale a României
IONESCU, ANAMARIA
　ZODIAC – A Noir Novel from Romania/Anamaria Ionescu – București:
Tritonic Books, 2019
　ISBN: 978-606-749-400-6

Publisher: BOGDAN HRIB
Translated into English by the author
Editors: QUENTIN BATES & MARINA SOFIA
Cover: ALEXANDRA BARDAN
Order no. 191/january 2019
Pass for Press: january 2019
Printed in Romania

Any reproduction of this work without the written permission of the publisher is strictly forbidden and is punishable under the Copyright Act..

Anamaria Ionescu

ZODIAC
A Noir Novel from Romania

CHAPTER ONE

Fat raindrops smacked against the windscreen as the wipers struggled to cope with the dirty mixture of mud and rain from the road. The heavy car seemed to have no trouble with the country road and Dragan was deeply proud of it. He had longed for an SUV from the day he had first held his new driving licence in his hand, but a long series of misfortunes kept on forcing him to postpone his dream. Now that the old man was gone, his inheritance had made his desire come true; a Wrangler Jeep in military green with every optional extra. Driving to work was no longer a chore, even in shitty weather like this.

It went without saying that he still had to work long hours, five days a week in that Godforsaken hole, sleeping in that lousy hut. But when he drove home on a Friday night, he at least knew what he was slaving away for; a car that he loved dearly and the most beautiful house in Voineasa. The house was the other achievement he was extremely proud of. When his father passed away, his cottage had two small rooms, a dank kitchen and a toilet in the back yard. Now he had a two-storey home, every up-to-date appliance, a big bathroom and anyone could see its big green roof, matching the forest behind, from every corner of the neighbourhood.

'Shit!'

Dragan glanced sideways at his colleague in the passenger seat, making a hopeless attempt to wipe clean a mayonnaise stain on the Jeep's dash.

'Fuck it, Vasile. I told you not to eat in the car.'

'C'mon, man, I was starving.'

Dragan muttered a few angry words and reached for the box of tissues. He reached it easily, but a bump in the road made him drop it. He fumbled for it, keeping a hand on the wheel. As his concentration lapsed, the Jeep swerved off the road and a second later its right tyre was in a ditch. As much as he tried to pull it clear, all he could hear was the sound of the front wheel digging itself deeper into the roadside mud.

'It's no use,' Dragan growled. 'We'll have to get out and see if we can dig it out. And throw that shit away or I'll make you swallow it, wrapper and all.'

For half an hour they tried to get the Jeep clear of the mud that held it tight. When it became obvious that they didn't have a chance in hell of had getting it out with their bare hands, they searched the undergrowth at the side of the road for logs that they could push under the wheels to provide some traction against the mud. Vasile found one that looked the right size and climbed up the pile to pull it free. He lost his footing and tumbled down in a clatter of wood and stones. Dazed, he made an effort to get to his feet. When he'd steadied himself, his eyes focused. What he saw next made him scream. The top of a man's head and one hand protruded from under the logs and stones.

*

Chief Inspector Marius Stanescu paced from one end of his office to the other, puffing smoke like a chimney. Anyone would expect that a senior post in the quiet police district of Sinaia, deep in the lush Prahova valley, packed with tourists for much of the year, would be as good as a session in a spa on the shores of Lake Amara. The truth was that most of the time it was a remarkably relaxed place for law and order. But every now and then something truly mind-boggling would crop up. He had never felt so frustrated in all of his twenty years of policing. Well, maybe that wasn't quite true. There had been that case five years ago, when an old man murdered that Catholic priest.

At least, back then he had been allowed to get on with his job and catch the criminal. Now the situation was unbelievably complex and he had been forbidden from interfering in a case in his own back yard. Less than forty-eight hours ago, a government official by the name of Sebastian Modrogan had been found dead in his hotel suite. He appeared to be have been poisoned and his much younger fiancée was nowhere to be found. His team dug out some juicy details about the official's private life, including that a year before his death divorce had put an end to twenty-five years of marriage. According to the tabloids, his young blonde chief of staff was the reason for him abandoning his wife. Bitter and ashamed, his former wife had hidden herself away in her home town of Voineasa.

He had been about to go for a trip up there himself to push the investigation forward when a heavyweight from Internal Affairs had marched into his office without knocking, flashing an ID that said his name was Branescu. The man had proceeded to slap a written order on his desk, confiscated the case notes and even the computer hard drives containing information about Modrogan's death. The inspector had tried to protest, but he'd been ignored.

That's why Marius was in his office, chain smoking in anger and frustration. Orders or no orders, he was a policeman and had no intention of backing off just because some officials were jittery about the way he carried out the investigation. But it looked like he had no choice. To hell with every one of them!

He got up and went to the filing cabinet in the corner of the room, took out a couple of files, felt for the bottle at the back and took a decent slug that helped dampen his fury. Back at his desk, he snatched the biggest envelope he could find, and stuffed the remaining case notes into it. In his haste to get the job done, he dropped a photo from the crime scene. He picked it up and took a look. For the life of him, he had no idea what this thing was all about, and most likely, he never would find out. He shrugged his shoulders and dropped the picture into the envelope with the other paperwork. Then he got up, yanked open the door and yelled.

'Vasilescule, rise and shine!'

A young man in uniform appeared.

'Somewhere down the hallway there's a clown from the Internal Affairs Administration who looks like an undertaker,' he said, handing him the envelope. 'Hand him this and tell him that I'll break his legs if he ever shows up again.'

*

'The old woman lay in the armchair, with the remote in one hand and the drink in the other. Well, she wasn't that old, but she'd been a heavy drinker and that had definitely taken its toll. And she wore a wig, a bright red one that had slipped incongruously sideways and looked ridiculous. Those open eyes and gaping mouth made me think of a fish on dry land. And, to crown it all, she had a mark on her forehead.'

'A mark?' his wife asked, looking up from setting the table.

'Yeah. Some sort of mark, like she was hit with something. Forensics couldn't identify it. What's for dinner? I'm as hungry as a wolf.'

The woman looked her husband in the eyes for a moment.

'It serves me right for marrying a cop and then having nothing better to do than to ask him how his day was. But to answer your question, we have schnitzel, mashed potatoes and sauerkraut salad.'

*

Lidia buried her face in her hands.

'Silviu, where the hell are you?'

She must have called him at least a dozen times in the last hour, both his mobile and his landline. The mobile went straight to voicemail, which told her it had to be switched off, and there was no answer on the home phone. Knowing there was a traffic camera at the end of Silviu's street, Lidia patched into the system and noticed that his car was parked outside his building. He could still be out, but he usually kept her informed of his whereabouts. They'd spoken in the morning and Silviu had mentioned that he was going to have a girl over for dinner. he'd even asked her for a recipe.

Lidia had spent a few hours searching for a new flat for him. After that little amorous encounter at his place, relocating him was mandatory. By the time she could feel her ankles swollen from sitting still and her eyes aching from staring at the screen, she'd decided it was time for a cup of tea to break the routine. Glancing at her watch, she then realised that she hadn't done the evening check-in with Silviu yet. He should have texted her a smiley face two hours ago. From that moment on, she'd been glued to the phone trying to reach him, but no luck. Now she was seriously worried.

She got up and strode to her colleague's desk at the other end of the room. Dragos was busy with a strategy game on his computer. Lidia placed a hand on his shoulder.

'Dragos, I need help…

'No problem. Talk to me.'

'It's Silviu. I can't reach him. He should have been in touch two hours ago. He's not answering his phone. His car is parked at his place, but he's nowhere to be seen.'

'Maybe he's watching a movie or something and lost track of time?'

'Doubt it. Last time we spoke he'd invited a girl over and was cooking dinner.'

'A girl? At his place? Lidia, this is not good.'

'Tell me about it! I'm already on the hunt for a new flat. But I have a bad feeling about this. I need to get to him and I can't drive…'

'Let's go,' Dragos said, sweeping up his coat and car keys in a single movement.

*

Lidia couldn't hold back the tears.

'It was my job to watch his back.'

'Lidia, stop it. It's not your fault,' Dragos said, trying to console her.

He could understand his colleague's despair. Their role was almost to be nannies to the agents in the field. They were supposed to gather information and anything else the agents needed to carry out their assignments, and that included providing as much protection as they could. Lidia had definitely screwed up.

Silviu's death triggered a whole series of headaches for the Agency. These agents were normally untraceable, as good as ghosts. Nobody was supposed to be able to find them, let alone kill them. Dragos was trying to calm Lidia down, but he was also trying to clear his mind of the image of the dead man. Unfortunately, it was now burnt into his retina. Silviu had died on the sofa in his flat, head lolling backwards, eyes open and his belly slashed wide open. Thank God that Manta, his own agent, was a disciplined operator, he reflected. Well, most of the time…

He told himself that most of the time Manta was perfectly capable of looking after himself. But the death of an agent raised an inevitable series of questions. Was the system secure? Were these people sufficiently hidden? Were they, the computer wizards, capable of providing covers and means of protection for the field agents?

Dragos almost wet himself when he felt a heavy hand on his shoulder. He turned and saw to his relief that it was one the team.

'Man, what the hell…?'

'Sorry, sir. I came to let you know the chief is here.'

'Branescu? Here?'

The puppetmaster himself was here, so this had to be worse than it looked. He felt sorry for Lidia. Dragos wanted to go out and meet the chief, but something made him stay. Although the thought of it made him sick, he steeled himself to run his eyes over the body lying on the sofa. There was something on the dead man's forehead. A sign of some sort.

*

The early spring was struggling to chase the winter away. Patches of snow coexisted with the green of the grass. Small and shy, spring mountain flowers made the place look fresh.

The statue of Prometheus holding the lightning bolt aloft reflected the rising sun, sending shafts of glittering artificial light to the four corners of the world from his regal position above the Vidraru dam. Sergiu stared at the rebel god's solid muscles for a few seconds, wiped the sweat from his brow with the towel around his neck and started to make his way down the stairs, struggling to get back into the old rhythm.

They'd brought him to this sleepy tourist resort at Vidraru for recovery. His last job ended up in something of a mess, more so than usual, and he'd barely made it out alive. He had shoulder and leg injuries that he was supposed to be recovering from now. After medical treatment, the Agency had decided he needed some rest and recuperation to get back on his feet, both physically and mentally. The place was pleasant and welcoming. It even had a pretty decent gym, and the landscape was simply breathtaking.

Sergiu Manta walked into the hotel lobby, glancing in passing at the welcome notice. He couldn't understand why They'd named the place The Valley with Fish. It was simply ridiculous. Manta set himself a strict routine; up at six, training beneath Prometheus' watchful gaze, shower, breakfast and a little flirting with the sweet blonde running the restaurant, then entertaining himself with movies, books, rowing on the lake, climbing the rocks. The problem was that he was bored to death. Although he wasn't going to admit it, he missed action.

He shook off his dark thoughts, put on a smile and searched out his favourite member of staff.

'Good morning, miss.'

'Mr. Manta, good morning. How was your morning run?'

'Fine. And hard work. Right now I could eat a horse.'

'I'll see to it. Your usual breakfast? There's fine weather so I'll set the table on the terrace. By the time you're done with your shower everything will be ready for you.'

'You really look after me. Thank you,' Sergiu said and elegantly kissed her hand. The girl instantly flushed bright red. He took a few steps towards the door, paused and turned back to her. 'Your hair looks nice this morning,' he said quietly and she flushed again, thin fingers going to her blonde curls.

An hour later, Sergiu regretfully left the terrace overlooking the lake just as the rain began to patter on the mosaic pavement. He ordered another Irish coffee, his eyes on the big screen over the bar. The news channel broke to a news bulletin, and one item was an accident that had taken place in a forest when a landslide had uncovered a hidden body. The two men who had stumbled across the corpse were clearly distressed as reporters kept pushing microphones into their faces. Sergiu frowned and looked for the remote to change the channel, but before he could find it, the bartender appeared.

'There's a call for you. You can take it in the office,' he said.

'Thank you,' Sergiu said and went to the room behind the bar that served as an office. 'Vacation over. Back to the job,' he whispered to himself before picking up the phone.

CHAPTER TWO

Sergiu closed his eyes and felt the wind caress his head, reminding him of riding a motorcycle in the past. On the roads he used a helmet, but when he took the forest paths near where he lived he had liked to feel the wind through his long hair. But that was in another life.

Now his hair was brush-cut, military style. It was easier this way.

He wondered why on earth Dragos had picked this convertible? The boy had no idea what discretion meant. He sneaked a sideways look. Dragos wasn't himself. This murder business had hit him hard.

The thing Sergiu couldn't understand was the connection that the Agency saw between the dead workman in the Voineasa forest, the poisoned minister in Sinaia, the old hag in Bucharest and their man. And what was he needed for? Those people were already dead.

He looked again at the youngster behind the wheel. He was noticeably tense.

'Dragos, are you all right, man?'

'I saw him. I saw Silviu dead. His head was hanging over the couch, eyes wide open. Like he was looking at me, and he had that shit on his forehead. Lidia was crying her heart out. I should have been there to look after her, but I couldn't take my eyes off the body. I felt sick, but I couldn't stop staring at him.'

'And Branescu showed up at the scene?' Sergiu asked, trying to steer the boy's mind away from the image of Silviu.

'Yes. He seemed really agitated. He made us keep internet communication at the minimum possible level. Several jobs were cancelled and agents recalled.'

From their point of view, Branescu was the big chief. He was the one who had recruited Sergiu. Well, maybe 'recruited' wasn't quite the right word. It had been the simple choice between a twenty-year jail sentence for double murder or doing some discreet killing in the national interest. If the chief was taking a personal interest, then things were probably way more serious than they looked.

'And what does he need me for?'

'He didn't say. He instructed me not to call your mobile and to pick you up personally.'

'Sorry, mate. After last night this trip must be hell for you. I can drive if you want.'

'Relax, I'm fine. Driving calms me down. If I get tired, we can switch.'

*

Sergiu, you got too used to the good life, he told himself, as he rubbed his eyes and laid his head against the table.

'Sleepy? So I did the right thing bringing these.' Branescu placed the two mugs of coffee on the table. Sergiu sipped at his gratefully. 'I have Dragos feeding data into the system to sort things out. He said it might take a while. We have time for coffee.'

'Can we go out on the terrace? I'd like to smoke.'

'Bad habit.'

'Somehow, I don't think smoking will be the death of me,' Sergiu smiled.

They sat in silence for a few moments. Sergiu took a black leather pouch from his pocket, busied himself with papers and tobacco as he rolled himself a cigarette. He lit it and took a puff before asking any questions.

'What's the situation with these murders? And why do you need me?'

'The death of state secretary Modrogan is alarming. The Sinaia police presumed that the guy's love life got to him. Then we found out about Silviu. There's a strong possibility that the two deaths are connected. It's too much of a coincidence. Modrogan died on Saturday. Three days later Silviu was killed.'

'And the other two victims?'

"A forester, sixty years old, killed near Voineasa. Two guys trying to get some timber found him. It caused a big fuss in the media.'

'I know. I saw it.'

'Then an elderly woman was found dead in her apartment in Dristor district in Bucharest.'

'I don't see the connection.'

'Neither did I at first. But the cop on the old woman's case looked for common elements with other murders. He started out in Bucharest. Then turned his attention to the victims' birthplaces.'

'Meaning every one of them was born in Voineasa? Really?'

'Yes. Silviu as well.'

'Shit...'

'There's another thing,' Branescu said, and paused. 'Each of the four victims seems to have a strange mark.'

'Including Silviu?'

'Yes.'

'Does this local cop know about our guy?'

'Not yet. But you'll tell him.'

'I'll tell him?'

'Yes. You'll be working together.'

'Working to… what?" Sergiu asked in surprise.

'To figure out who's behind all this, of course. I checked him. He's a good cop. Intuitive. A little too intuitive.'

'What am I supposed to be doing?'

'You assist him. Help out with useful information, stuff that we're already certain of. Keep an eye on him. Report anything he discovers. We have to find out how the killer got to our agent. Finally, the most important thing, you finish him off before he gets to be interrogated by the police, prosecution or anyone else.'

'What if there are more than one?'

'More than one what?'

'Murderers. We can't rule that possibility out.'

'Then you take them all out,' Branescu said coldly, picking up his phone as it buzzed for a second. 'Well, let's go. Your new partner has arrived.'

Sergiu smiled briefly. Branescu caught that and looked at him with a silent question in his eyes.

'I usually kill. Now I hunt killers. It's an interesting change.'

'Don't get used to it. Once this circus is over, it's back to business as usual.'

*

Gentle afternoon light filtered through the office windows. Sergiu and Chief Inspector Marius could hear the faint noises of Bucharest traffic coming from below as they discussed the murders.

'Look! It's already gone five…' Dragos said. The other two raised their heads from the files thy were reading.

'Any plans?' Sergiu asked with a smile. 'Are we cramping your style?'

'Well, sort of … I didn't know this was going to take so long. And I have a date…'

'How long did you expect a murder investigation to take?' Sergiu asked with a touch of sarcasm.

'With a supercop like Marius on our side? Twenty minutes at the most,' Dragos replied, winking at the policeman, who nodded and gave him a thin smile.

'What do you say we give the boy a break?' Marius suggested. 'Let him make a girl happy.'

'Or deeply unhappy,' Sergiu said. 'Go on, enjoy yourself. We'll look after your workload.'

'You're sure you'll manage?' Dragos asked, with a worried look at the computers and array of devices scattered across the conference table.

'Well, if we break anything today, then you can fix it tomorrow.'

Dragos scratched his head. He kept forgetting that Sergiu Manta had been an IT specialist himself in another life, and a good one, too. Without a word he got his stuff and was gone.

'Thanks a lot, guys!' they heard him call from along the corridor.

'Strange kid,' Marius said.

'Yeah, but he's all right.'

'How did you end up working together?'

'Our lord and master decided,' Sergiu replied with a nod of his head in the direction of Branescu's office.

Marius had plenty of questions on his mind but held back from asking them. This was a completely new situation for him. He had tried to dig deeper into the murder of an old lady and he ended up involved in the investigation of a series of killings, including that of a government official, in partnership with a hush-hush agency belonging to Internal Affairs that nobody would tell him anything about. This guy, Sergiu, seemed all right, but he didn't have much to say about himself either, or about his colleague's death. Marius had only just got to hear about this final death.

On the other hand, this Sergiu seemed to be very good at asking questions. In just two hours, he had learned that Marius was married, that his wife was from Istanbul, that her name was Meryam, which signified stubbornness or persistence, and the name suited her perfectly. Marius had also let fall that they were expecting a child and that he hoped for a bonus after solving this case, because their living costs were sky-high. And all that in just two hours... The cop's train of thought was interrupted by a chirp of his mobile phone. Sergiu looked at him.

'It's my wife,' Marius said. 'She's asking if I'll be home for dinner.'

'Well, go then. She's pregnant, leaving her all alone isn't a great idea.'

'Is that the voice of experience? You have a family as well?'

Sergiu should have anticipated this line of questioning. Nevertheless, he felt been caught out. He could feel his face flush and was pretty sure it hadn't gone unnoticed.

'I had,' he answered briefly and suddenly his throat went dry.

'What happened?'

'They are not ... here any longer.'

Liar, Marius found himself thinking, not knowing where that thought had come from.

'I'm sorry...,' he said.

'Don't be. Go home. Tomorrow we'll pick up where we left off.'

'What do you reckon we should start with?'

Sergiu shrugged.

'Let's start with what's at hand. The Bucharest murder. The lady in Dristor.'

'Yeah, that makes sense. See you tomorrow.'

'Sure,' Sergiu replied.

Marius headed for the door, tucking his shirt in as he went. Since he'd started piling on the weight, his shirts kept coming adrift. His wife said he looked like a recycled clerk with a hangover. Speaking of which, it was time to call her.

'Always call before going home,' he recalled his father saying. 'No use breaking a marriage over a phone call, is it?'

*

Once alone, Sergiu closed his eyes for a few moments. Then he went to the espresso machine and punched the buttons that would give him a coffee.

He took an iPod from his pocket and connected it to the loudspeakers in the room. The opening notes of System of a Down's *Aerials* filled the room. He opened the window wide and lit a cigarette. After few puffs he went back to the files spread across the table. He dragged the whiteboard over to where he was sitting, telling himself that it was time to test whether the whodunit movie cliché had any truth in it. He drew columns for each murder and added data for every one of them.

The first column was for the first victim, Vasile Petrache, the forester whose body was discovered near the road in Voineasa. Age sixty-two. Death had occurred, according to the post-mortem, a month before, probably in February. The body, or what was left of it, showed the marks of several heavy blows with a blunt object, a baseball bat or something of that nature. The decisive blow was the one at the base of the man's skull. Because of the disturbed surroundings at the scene, it was difficult to say whether he had been killed there or not. Investigations had shown that the last sighting of Vasile Petrache had been on St John's Day, the seventh of January, when he drank himself unconscious in one of the town's bars. Nobody had noticed his absence. As the dead man had no family, nobody had reported him missing.

Next was Modrogan, the minister. Aged forty-seven and divorced after twenty-five years of marriage.

Dragos had added some newspaper clippings that told the story of something of a dedicated ladies' man. Nevertheless, in terms of financial arrangements, he had been more than fair to his former wife. The media had announced his engagement to his chief of staff, a blonde of twenty-seven with an economics degree. However, at the time of his death, the two of them had been spending a little time apart. She was currently on a shopping spree in Milan, which made it difficult to track her down. Modrogan had died in his hotel room in Sinaia. He had checked in there in company of a brunette who was likewise nowhere to be found. The murder had been carried out with poison added to a glass of wine. His right cheek bore the mark of a blow that had been administered while he was still alive. According to the forensic pathologist, this had most likely been a blow from a fist, also leaving a semi-circular mark that nobody had yet been able to identify. Modrogan's body had been found by hotel staff on the morning of the third of March. Death had most likely occurred the previous evening between ten and midnight, although the final report was not yet ready.

Then there was Silviu, their agent. He died three days later in his rented apartment, provided by the Agency. The murder weapon was most likely a sharp kitchen carving knife, which was not found at the crime scene. The body bore a round mark on its forehead, administered post-mortem. Sergiu had asked

Branescu to allow him access to the reports concerning Silviu's recent missions. This hadn't been approved, and even if Branescu were to give him access, this would be information he couldn't share with Marius.

The final victim was the old woman in Bucharest. Marius had described how they found her lying on the armchair, strangled with a pair of stockings. Elena Popescu had the same circular mark on her forehead. There was still no autopsy report available, but death had occurred, most likely, before Silviu's and Modrogan's.

Sergiu added the victims' photos to the columns on the board. Then he took a step back to see the full picture. Something was bothering him, but at first he couldn't put his finger on it. Then it came to him; it was the first victim, the forester. The state of the body, after lying in the mountains for so long, raised more questions than answers. It was clear the fatal blow had been the one to the back of the head, but apart from that it was virtually impossible to determine what had happened. So what had prompted Marius to include him in this series of killings? What was the connection? What was the connection between all the murders for that matter?

'Fuck me...' Sergiu murmured.

*

'Hurry up with that hot chocolate. I promised Grandma and Grandpa that we'll be there before lunch.'

'Did you tell Grandma to cook sarmale?' asked the boy with the Asian features, slurping noisily at his drink.

Unlike most kids his age, this one seemed keen on his cabbage leaves stuffed with pork.

'Drink properly, don't fool around!' the boy's mother said harshly. She was petite, with long curly hair, fashionably dyed in two colours. 'Grandma doesn't run a restaurant, so you'll eat whatever they put in front of you, and don't go fussing and making more work for the poor woman. Understood?'

'Yes, mum,' the boy replied with a sly smile. He had already decided he would text his grandmother once they got in the car.

From the opposite corner of the coffee shop, Sergiu was watching them, hidden behind a biker magazine. The woman and the child belonged to his former life. Life before prison, before becoming one of the Agency's ghosts for doing dirty jobs. He had officially been dead for some time. But that didn't stop him from keeping track of his wife and son and what went on in their lives. Dany was at school now. Once a month they would spend a weekend with the Mantas, Sergiu's adoptive parents. And every time they left for the mountain village of Codlea not far from Brasov, they had a habit of stopping at a service station coffee shop in Baneasa on the outskirts of Bucharest, where Dany had a hot chocolate and Maia a latte and a croissant. Whenever he could manage it, Sergiu would hide in corner of the place so that he could get a glimpse of them. It was risky, but he counted on the fact that they would never expect him to be there, so they were most likely to ignore a guy having a quiet coffee. Sergiu disguised himself by wearing a mechanic's overalls and with a cap covering half of his face. With grease on his hands and a petrol-soaked rag hanging from one pocket, Sergiu hid behind the magazine, enjoying every word that passed between his son and his wife. He noticed with pride that Dany had gained a few inches, while Maia had lost a few kilos and looked magnificent. He wasn't entirely sure about the two-tone hair, but reminded himself it was none of his business.

He listened with interest to his son's account of a motorbike he had last seen with his grandfather in the tourist resort of Poiana Brasov.

'It was a Harley, but it was bigger than Dad's. It was dark blue and had wolves painted all over it. It was so cool!'

Sergiu began to feel so overcome with emotion that he almost forgot to turn the pages of the magazine.

'Mum, can I ask the mechanic guy over there to let me take a look at his magazine? I don't have that issue.'

Now Sergiu began to panic.

'No, you can't,' the boy's mother said. 'For one, because you shouldn't disturb people. And two, we need to go. We'll buy it when we get there.'

'Promise?'

'Yes.'

Maia paid and helped Dany into his jacket. The boy took a last noisy slurp from his cup and put the buds of his iPod in his ears. It was the same device with a cracked display that Sergiu had with him in prison. He watched the car leave the parking and then relaxed. He had been so close to blowing it. He would have to find a less obvious observation point.

*

'You're late,' Marius said, a broad smile on his face.

Of course he was. After seeing his wife and son at the coffee shop, Sergiu had gone home, changed out of his mechanic's outfit, had another coffee and a smoke to calm his nerves. It was almost eleven o'clock when he got back to headquarters.

'Like an aristocrat,' Dragos commented from behind the computer.

'What can I say, kiddo? Not all of us are chased out of bed by the ladies when morning comes,' Sergiu grinned.

Marius laughed.

'Relaxed? Ready to work?'

'Definitely. I took another look through the files last night and I have a question. How did you connect the murders?'

'What do you mean?' Marius asked, looking serious.

'What made you think they were carried out by the same perpetrator, or perpetrators?'

The policeman scratched his right ear. The truth was that he relied on two common elements: that the victims all shared the same birthplace in Voineasa, and the peculiar mark that had been left on each face. The problem was that they still didn't know how the marks had been made. The object used was definitely circular, like some sort of a stamp. Of course, the same birthplace for all the victims could hardly be a coincidence. In fact, Marius had been doubtful about this, but once he found out about Silviu, the secret victim, who fitted in perfectly with the others, those doubts had gone.

Sergiu listened carefully to Marius explain, with a forefinger pressed to his lips.

'The first victim, the guy found near the road, you know … the body is so degraded that it's impossible to tell if he had the round mark or not. So in that case, half of your reasoning is out.'

'It wasn't really a deduction – more of an instinct. And if I'm right, then there are more common elements between these murders still to be found. Of course, we could be talking about a serial killer. But the thinking is that the modus operandi should have been pretty much the same for all murders. The most likely factor is that these people were killed for a reason. We have to work with what's in front of us. The number of murders may be limited. No more killings – no more new clues to work with.'

'That's a cynical point of view,' Dragos said.

'But realistic,' Marius replied.

'Well, I don't know,' Sergiu said, thinking aloud. "Let's say that this second factor is correct. How do we know there won't be more killings?'

'We don't,' Marius admitted. 'But, in the end, how many people can be at war with each other at the same time?'

Sergiu scratched his head, as if looking for something that wasn't there any more. He looked at the board with the details of the murders, stood close to it and took down one of the pictures. It was the photo of Silviu's face, grim in death. Sergiu looked at it with a frown as he ran his fingers through his red brush-cut hair.

*

Marius agreed right away when Sergiu suggested a visit to the apartments of the two Bucharest victims whose homes were also the crime scenes. Marius liked to examine a victim's home as there was no telling what interesting angles that could open. Plus, this gave him an opportunity to check out the place where Sergiu's deceased colleague had lived.

Silviu Voinescu's death was as much of a mystery as his life had been. Marius had been trying to look him up in the official records but there was no mention of him anywhere. He even tried a search in the Internal Affairs database he had clearance for. Nada! Legally, the man simply did not exist. His social security number was false; the ministry's human resources department had never heard of him and the police had no information whatsoever. The guy didn't own a car, didn't have a bank account, didn't pay any taxes and had no debts or tickets for that matter. Marius was tempted to ask Sergiu about it, but decided to hold back for the moment. He intended to do a thorough search on his new partner as well, although his gut feeling told him he would not get much out of it.

When they got out of the car, the rain was barely a drizzle but the wind had picked up. Elena Popescu's residence was in the Dristor district of the city, in a building on the main boulevard. Dristor district was one of the most fashionable areas of Bucharest with plenty of shops and the IOR park close by. They found the entrance, squeezed between a coffee shop and a convenience store. First thing that hit Sergiu as they entered was the smell of damp cloth. He couldn't understand why cleaners didn't change the water in their buckets more often. Everything looked clean enough, but if you closed your eyes and breathed in deeply, you had the feeling that might expect to find a dead rat under your feet.

The studio flat was spacious, but filled with decrepit old furniture. They opened the four wardrobe doors, all packed with clothes that had long been out of fashion. Sergiu went through a few drawers stuffed with bills, receipts and pension paperwork. There was a jewel case by the bed, full of cheap stuff. The only jewellery of any value was a gold chain and a thin wedding ring, as well as a pair of silver earrings in the shape of four-leaf clovers that had been carefully placed in a red heart-shaped box. Sergiu assumed the old lady must have received these as a present at some point, or else she intended them as a present for someone else.

A stack of unopened mail lay on a small table by the window and Sergiu checked through the bills. A credit recovery firm was already chasing her for an unpaid phone bill. He picked up the receiver of the antique rotary phone and put it to his ear. As he had expected, there was no dial tone.

'Not so good with money. She had debts,' he muttered to himself.

Based on what they could find in the house, there had been no robbery. The woman simply had hardly anything to tempt a thief.

Marius went into the kitchen and wrinkled his nose at the smell.

'Rancid,' he said, glaring at the oil in the frying pan.

The kitchen was filthy, with a palpable layer of grease on the walls and furnishings. But the gas stove and the fridge looked new; surprisingly so. Marius opened the fridge to find an opened bottle of sparkling water, a beer, six eggs in a carton and some raw chicken on a small plate. He opened the cutlery drawer. Knives and forks were neatly arranged, but tarnished. He was about to close the drawer when he noticed a piece of paper under the kitchen knives. He pulled it free and found an envelope in his hand.

'Sergiu, come and see!'

Between them, they emptied the envelope's contents onto the table. There were a few old photos; a man in workman's overalls, a woman in a floral dress

– presumably a very young Elena Popescu – an elderly man and woman, a little girl clasping a stuffed bear, and a birth certificate. Amalia Dresda, born on the eighth of August 1980, in Voineasa. Mother: Elena Dresda. Father: unknown.

'Voineasa again,' Marius said.

'And Elena Popescu is the mother? Than why is the name Dresda on the certificate? And where the hell is this girl? Don't we have to inform her of her mother's death? Didn't you guys look into it? How come these came up just now?'

Marius was embarrassed that he hadn't done his job as thoroughly as he should have.

'I admit we didn't pay much attention to this place. I was pretty sure there wasn't much to be found here. The feeling was that this was an attempted burglary gone bad.'

'Look, pal,' Sergiu said, gesturing to the photos and papers on the table. 'Even so, this is not OK.'

'No, far from it,' Marius said, and deciding that he needed to let his police partner Dumitru have a piece of his mind next time they met.

The night they had found the victim, while conducting the search of the flat, Marius received a phone call from his mother. His sister, Alina, had sneaked out of the house to go to the mountains with some bastard. This was an old story repeating itself. His sister had been secretly going out with a boy involved in selling stolen cars. Marius and his parents had warned her off seeing him again, but at eighteen, the girl was as stubborn as any mule, and besotted with her low-life boyfriend. Marius had dropped everything as the family crisis unfolded and ran for the station to catch his crazy sister, while Dumitru promised to keep handle everything. But, for obvious reasons, Marius didn't feel like telling Sergiu this story.

They took one more look around the flat and locked it behind them as they left, taking the photos and the certificate. In the car, Marius noticed Sergiu was carefully studying one of the photos.

'What have you seen?'

'This guy in the overalls. He looks familiar, but I can't tell where from.'

'Do you think it has anything to do with the case?'

'Well, what else?'

Marius shrugged, then stamped hard on the brakes. A startled dog scampered furtively across the street, ears flattened to his head.

*

'Your man lived here long?' Marius asked, browsing through the items scattered on the sideboard.

'No. Couple of months. He worked out of town for a long time,' Sergiu answered briefly.

'I thought so. It doesn't look like he made much of a home of this place.'

Sergiu was convinced there was little to be found in Silviu's apartment. But Marius wanted to visit it, naturally.

He was thinking about what Marius had said about Silviu's home not having a personal touch. Neither did his. It was the Agency's policy to move the agents from one place to another quite frequently. That way they couldn't put down any roots. Sometimes Sergiu longed for a place of his own. He remembered when he had the wooden cabin at Lasita, near Brasov. He lived near a forest, had a dog and felt free. That time seemed so far away...

'It must have been quite a shock to see him dead. No wonder the lad didn't want to come with us,' Marius said, distracting Sergiu from his thoughts. Marius compared the couch in the living room where Silviu had been found, and the photos taken by forensics.

Dragos had firmly declined the offer to accompany his colleagues in their visits to the victims' home. The keyboard wizard hadn't recovered from the shock of seeing Silviu's body.

Sergiu was right. There was nothing to be found in the dead agent's home.

'Do we know his plans for that evening?'

'He told his partner he was having a girl over. He even asked her what to cook.'

'And what did he cook?'

'Nothing,' Sergiu said. 'He ordered from La Mama.'

'Tasteful, getting his date a meal from a restaurant chain. Does his partner know anything about the girl?'

'No. Nothing at all.'

'Too bad. OK, I'm done. Let's go, there's nothing in here.'

Marius sighed, scratched his ear and made for the door. Sergiu took another look around the room. He was about to follow Marius when he noticed something white on the floor, half under the sofa. Sergiu bent down and picked up the scrap of paper, glanced at it and put it in his pocket.

The two of them made their way in silence down the echoing stairwell.

'Did you say he ordered food from La Mama?' Marius asked suddenly.

'That's right.'

'Did anyone think to try and get in touch with the delivery guy?'

'Hmmm … thinking like a cop, aren't you?' Sergiu said and grinned.

'I am? Really?'

*

Although unlikely to turn up anything new, Marius asked to talk to Lidia, the IT specialist who was Silviu's office-based partner. As Sergiu had predicted, she didn't have much to add. she'd already told them everything she knew. 'Talking' was something of a misnomer, since Lidia did little more than cry her heart out, to the extent that Marius almost regretted asking to speak to her. No new information popped up, and Marius found himself virtually paralysed in the presence of a distraught woman. He had no idea what to do, and neither did the agent at his side.

'Had Silviu been behaving oddly lately? Did he do anything out of the ordinary?'

'No, he didn't,' the girl said, blowing her nose. 'Except for drawing those circle things.'

'Circle things?'

'Yeah. Whenever he had to think, or if something was bothering him, he'd doodle, all sorts of shapes, but recently he kept drawing those weird circles.'

'A strange mannerism...' Marius said, silently wondering this was normal behaviour for agents. In fact, what kind of agents were they? What were these guys doing? He had asked questions here and there, but nobody could tell him anything about the agency. Most people didn't even know it existed.

'A circle like this one?' Sergiu asked, bringing Marius back to reality.

He took a small piece of paper from his pocket and showed it to the girl.

'Yes, something like that. Different kind of drawing, though...'

Marius took the paper and looked at it carefully. It was torn out from a school notebook. The drawing looked like the ones children do, when they place a coin under the paper and use a pencil to imprint the pattern on it. This particular coin must have had some markings, as the image came out poorly and a few holes had been torn in the paper.

'Thanks, Lidia,' Sergiu said. 'Dragos, walk her to her desk and make sure she's all right.'

'Where did this come from?" the policeman asked holding up the scrap of paper up and looking into Sergiu's eyes.

'In Silviu's apartment. It was near the couch. I almost missed it.'

'And you just picked it up...?'

'Yes.'

'And so any prints on it go down the fucking drain,' Marius snapped.

'It didn't cross my mind. I'm afraid I don't have a copper's mind,' Sergiu replied.

Marius sighed, frustrated that he had missed the paper himself.

'I need some fresh air,' he said, banging the door behind him as he left the room.

In the meantime, Dragos had returned and had heard part of the conversation. Now he was looking at Sergiu in confusion. Sergiu took the paper left on the desk and handed it to Dragos.

'Get it checked. Fingerprints.'

'But Marius just said...'

'Never mind what Marius said. You do what I tell you to. Check if there are any fingerprints apart from mine, the mad policeman's and Silviu's, OK? And whatever you find, you bring it to me, got it?'

'Got it.'

Sergiu had intentionally compromised any potential prints. Although they were supposed to be working on this investigation with the police, any results were for the Agency's eyes only. There would be no trial.

Dragos left the room. Once alone, Sergiu remembered the photos and the certificate they had found in the old lady's apartment. He opened the envelope and took out the picture that had caught his eye earlier in the day. He examined it for a while, then took a magnifying glass and studied the man's face. After that he placed the photo on the board. When a calmer Marius returned, he found Sergiu with a smile on his face.

'All right?' Sergiu asked in reply to the unasked question in Marius' eyes. 'Come here, I want to show you the proof of your unquestionable policeman's instinct. Remember the photos we took from the old woman's place?'

He placed the picture he had just studied near the photo of the first victim, the man found in the forest. Then he handed him the magnifying glass with an extravagant gesture. Marius took it and studied the two photos for a while. They had clearly been taken years apart. But apart from that, it was also clear that they showed the face of the same man. There was a connection between two of the victims at least, supporting the theory that Marius had put forward.

'Well, well. It seems I'm pretty good at this,' Marius told Sergiu, with a satisfaction he didn't try to hide.

CHAPTER THREE

'Woman, leave me be! I'm having a beer with my son. It's not like we do drugs or anything. It's called bonding. Fathers and sons do that in the civilised world.'

Every time she heard that speech, Sergiu's adoptive mother would roll her eyes in despair. The Mantas had adopted the boy when he was already a teenager, which precluded any traditional parent-child relationship. Corneliu Manta chose instead to adopt the role of an older friend, a mentor for the youthful rebel. Once the boy had turned sixteen, the two of them would occasionally go for a beer, as men do. His wife, Tamara, didn't mind them going out together. But for the life of her, she couldn't accept the idea that the boy was drinking beer at sixteen.

'He has a whole lifetime ahead of him to make friends with booze,' she growled.

Corneliu responded with one-liners lifted from American movies. Hollywood had enriched his vocabulary with a few transatlantic expressions that sounded incongruous coming from him. That was where the bonding idea had come from.

Thirty years later Sergiu was bonding all over again; this time with this strange cop who looked like he had been blown in by a storm. He came across as a good-humoured, clever kind of guy. Too clever and too intuitive for his own good, Sergiu thought. At first, Sergiu had politely declined to go for a drink with Marius.

In his former life, he'd been friends with a military policeman. Cristian Herra was part of the murder investigation team, he'd investigated the very murders that sent Sergiu to prison for twenty years – the same crimes that had made Sergiu's recruitment possible.

Cristian Herra and Sergiu had met under difficult circumstances, but their friendship had been an honest one that ran deep. So much so, that Herra had been discharged from the police for having tried to help Sergiu get away with it. In addition, Cristian Herra was one of the very few who knew that Sergiu Manta's death had been staged, after which he had become a ghost agent for an obscure department of Internal Affairs. That knowledge was to cost him his life.

Sergiu didn't want any more dead friends. But, in the end, he had no choice but to accept his new partner's repeated invitation. He couldn't keep on finding polite excuses to turn him down. On the other hand, Branescu had made it plain that he wanted him to get into the policeman's mind, as he put it.

To make things worse, Sergiu was beginning to develop a real liking for Marius Stanescu. He enjoyed listening to his stories about the domestic squabbles with Meryem, about the guys at the police station, about the cases they had pulled off. Needing some stories of his own, Sergiu told him about his childhood in an orphanage in Brasov, how he had been adopted just as everyone had given up on him, about the relationship with his adoptive parents. These were stories from the past, that wouldn't provide the policeman any information about the present. The trouble was that these confidences opened the door to a new friendship, and that was the last thing Sergiu Manta needed.

*

'Shit…' Marius growled.

He had spent two hours searching police databases and pestering colleagues for information. All in vain. he'd found nothing of any use. His eyes ached from staring at the screen. He stretched, yawned and rubbed his temples.

'Do you have a cigarette?'

Dragos popped his face over his own monitor.

'You smoke?' he asked in surprise.

'Not often, but yes. Occasionally.'

'Meaning you cadge smokes but don't pay for them.'

'That's one way of putting it.' Marius laughed. 'I get the urge to smoke when I'm on edge.'

'On edge? Why?'

'It's Amalia Dresda, the one we think could be Elena Popescu's daughter. We have a record of her birth then of her first seven school years. Then she vanishes without trace. There's nothing on her.'

'Could she be dead?'

'Then her death certificate would have been held by the authorities at her place of birth. That's the law. Unless…' Marius said and scratched his head.

'Unless she died God knows where and her body was never found. Or people around her had no idea who she really was?'

'Or the blasted woman's just very keen to stay hidden.'

'Why's it so important to find her?'

'Her birth certificate and her photo, together with a photo of another of the victims were all found in another victim's home. Both logic and my guts tell me

Amalia is the child of those two victims. That's why we have to find her.'

Marius sighed, stretched and looked around the room. He glanced over towards Sergiu's desk.

'Where's our super-agent?'

'No idea. He called and said there's something he needs to do.'

'What?'

'No idea. I didn't ask and Sergiu didn't say.'

'Isn't that just great? I'm working like a slave and he takes a walk. You can call him and tell him to get here right away.'

'Be my guest,' Dragos said with a sideways look. 'I'm too fond of life.'

'Who's afraid of the big bad wolf, big bad wolf, big bad wolf?' Marius chanted with a sarcastic grin.

Suddenly, Sergiu was right there in the room with them with a cheerful look on his face. Marius did a double take. The Sergiu he had got to know was a silent, serious type, with the whole weight of the world resting on his shoulders. But the man standing in front of him now had a smile on his lips and a look in his eyes that showed he clearly wanted to be let in on the joke.

'So, do you want to tell me?' he asked. 'Who's afraid of the big bad wolf?'

'Your young keyboard warrior here was asked to summon you to work. But he didn't want to catch a tiger by the tail.'

'A tiger, Dragos?' Sergiu asked with a smile.

'That's not what I said,' Dragos replied. 'I said I'm too fond of life.'

'That's something different.'

Marius frowned. 'So, where have you been wandering all morning?'

'I haven't been wandering. I call it working.'

Sergiu put a hand into one of the inside pockets of his biker jacket and extracted a ring, made in silver and adjustable so that it could fit any finger. It featured a round disc with two concentric circles engraved on it, with the signs of the zodiac between them and in the centre was a sun with unequal rays. Sergiu twisted it between his fingers and spun it in the ashtray on the desk. Dragos and Marius waited for it to stop spinning. When it did, Marius picked it up and studied it.

'So what is this?'

'It's the stamp used to make the round mark on our victims.'

For a moment Marius stared at Sergiu, wide-eyed. Then he slipped off his seat and hurried over to the magnetic board to compare the ring against the marks on the victims in the forensic photos.

'Fuck me. It looks like you got this one right...'

*

Phone to his ear, Marius Stanescu talked as he walked along the hallway, gesticulating with his free hand. There was no hiding his chagrin, although he made an effort to remain calm. He was trying hard to make a point, but with limited success, while Sergiu stood in the doorway and enjoyed the show.

His mobile had rung just as Sergiu had been explaining his discovery of the ring that had left its mark on the victims. He had uploaded the forensic photos to his computer then scanned the drawing on the piece of paper found in Silviu's apartment. From there, he had used software that overlaid the images onto each other and combined them to reveal a complete representation of the mark.

The final image was not highly detailed, and it wasn't even complete. But it had been enough to give him an idea of what the complete image might look like. After two hours of positioning and rotating the images, Sergiu had a disc with the sun in the middle and two strings of graphics around it. These were separated by two circles and twelve lines converging to the sun. He enhanced the image and pored over the graphics, until he realised that it was a zodiac. Sergiu searched online for similar images and quickly stumbled across the webpage of a place selling rock clothing and accessories. The funny thing was that back when he had lived in Brasov, he had bought Gotica's stuff. They were mainly an online store, but they did have a shop in the centre of Bucharest. Sergiu knew as soon as he saw the address that it had to be behind the old CEC bank on Victory Boulevard, one of the city centre's iconic buildings, known to everyone as the CEC Palace. The architect They'd brought in from France to build it back in the nineteenth century had made it look like a castle, complete with four towers and plenty of carved decoration, topped by a glass-and-metal dome.

On Mircea Voda Street he went straight to the shop, tucked away between the old-style houses that lined both sides of the narrow one-way street. The place seemed to be deserted. The shabby blinds and the stickers covering the window made it look closed. He tried the door anyway and it was open. Behind the counter he found a pretty girl with a Mireille Mathieu hair style, although dyed green.

'Hello, Laura,' he said, a flashback from a past life helping him make an impression. It was a gamble, but worth a risk. Back in the day, Sergiu had bulk ordered for himself and his friends in Brasov, and negotiated discounts. The girl would recognise him as a regular customer. There was every chance this could backfire on him, given his present line of work. But Sergiu decided the risk was worth taking and hoped that a relaxed chat would tell him what he needed to know.

He was able to establish that the ring paired with a matching pendant of the same design. Gotica silver jewellery was exclusive and rather expensive. So they had imported only five pairs to test the market. Three of them had been bought online. Laura provided Sergiu with the email addresses that the orders had come from. Another pair had been bought by two girls, twin sisters. One of them got the ring, the other one got the pendant. The last one had been bought by a man not long before the winter holiday. Laura remembered him because he was hardly a typical customer. He had been wearing a suit and tie, and his car had a driver. He paid cash. A couple of months later the press was full of Modrogan's untimely death and Laura realised who the mystery customer had been back in the middle of December.

'Did you say anything to the police?'

'What was there to say? The man did some Christmas shopping here,' Laura retorted. 'So what? I figured it had nothing to do with it. And if it did, you guys would come asking questions. And I was right.'

Sergiu asked her if she knew who the jewellery had been intended for, and the girl shrugged.

'Do you have any of these still in stock?' he asked, expecting her to shake her head.

Instead it turned out that Laura had kept a ring for herself, but had no problem selling it to Sergiu, providing him with something for the lab team to compare against the marks on the victims' bodies.

Now he waited patiently for Marius to finish his phone conversation so that they could see how this development might fit into their investigation. Sergiu felt that things were increasingly pointing towards a female assassin.

Finally, Marius stabbed at the phone's display, putting an end to the conversation.

'Sorry... My wife...'

'Everything OK?'

'Yeah. It's just that an idiot cousin of mine is celebrating his birthday, not that it's anything worth celebrating. He knows I'm not inclined to spend any time with him, so he talked to my wife. Meryem is sensitive about anything concerning the family, since her people are in Istanbul and not happy about us being married. They don't talk to her too often. In fact, they don't talk at all, so she has adopted my family. Including the bastards.'

Sergiu smiled.

'A wife's happiness is priceless. For anything else we have Mastercard,' he said, paraphrasing the old TV ad that everyone knew.

'Mastercard my arse,' Marius growled.

*

Sergiu saved anything related to the enquiry on a laptop and was absorbed in it. Although neither he nor Marius were looking forward to it, it was high time for them to go to Voineasa. Whatever connected the victims had to be found there.

Marius was trying hard to convince his sister to move into his place while he was away, at least for a few days. He felt sick at the prospect of leaving Meryem all by herself, only three months before the baby was due. He also hoped that taking care of his wife would keep his sister from seeing the bastard she had got herself involved with, the one who had caused Marius to mess up the search in the Dristor apartment.

'This trip couldn't come at a worse moment.'

'I'm not crazy about it either. Your sister didn't agree?

'She did. But I'll bet she'll wait for Meryem to fall asleep, then she'll be off to meet her lousy boyfriend. For the life of me, I don't understand what girls see in boys like that.'

'I wouldn't complain if I were you. If women didn't fall for bad boys, how on earth would it have been possible for a guy like you to get Meryem?'

'Aren't we funny today? Well, if you must know, I was a real gentleman. Hell, I still am,' Marius said and looked affronted as Dragos burst out laughing. 'Mister Apostolescu, your attitude offends me,' he said, trying hard to maintain a serious expression on his face.

'Mister Apostolescu, get us a car,' Sergiu broke in. 'An SUV, not one of those convertibles you like to play with, and I need an internet modem. While you're at it, I also need a contact in the local police force up there. Make sure you find someone with a brain in his head.'

'Consider it done,' Dragos said, sipping off his chair. He stopped in the doorway and turned. 'I almost forgot. The guys at the lab checked the piece of paper with the drawing you found at Silviu's place.'

Sergiu took his eyes off the computer screen and gave him a hard look.

'And?'

'Nothing important. They identified your prints, Marius's and Silviu's. There were a couple more, but there's no match on file.'

'It was unlikely to be much use. You put it in your

pocket, not in an evidence bag. The paper changed hands too many times. Even if we found something, it would have been compromised.'

'All the same, if it had linked to someone on the police database, then it would have at least given us a start,' Sergiu said with a humourless smile.

Dragos hurried from the room. He had caught the look on Sergiu's face. It had been made plain that whatever was found on that piece of paper was for his eyes only. Dragos knew he had put a foot badly wrong.

*

Oktoberfest was his favourite bar. It was the place that reminded him the most of Brasov and his old life. It was slightly trashy, lots of wood, quirky posters on the walls, rock music, and the beer was cheap. It was located in the city centre, making it easy to reach, and most important of all it was open around the clock. Sergiu was sat at the counter by the big window and looked out at the classier bar on the other side of the street. The huge signboard outside the Finnish Club changed colours every few seconds, from blue to pink, then through yellow, purple, green, and back to blue. Sergiu looked at the place's entrance and saw there was a girl with red hair and big blue eyes handing out flyers to passers-by. He appreciated her curves, especially the swell of her tits that he couldn't stop himself admiring. It was a cold evening and the air was filled with a mist of fine drizzle, so Sergiu could almost hear her teeth chattering through the glass. Their eyes met and the girl gave him a big beautiful smile. Sergiu passed a hand through his buzz-cut hair and smiled back at her.

He saw Dragos come through the door, so he switched his attention from the flyer girl with the tits to his colleague.

'I'm up for another beer. What are you having?'
'The same.'

Sergiu lifted a finger, smiled at the waitress, and she brought them two beers. Dragos sipped, and decided it was time to take the plunge.

'I'm sorry about earlier ... I shouldn't have mentioned the prints in front of Marius.

'No, you shouldn't have.'

'I know, but we are on the same team and I thought...'

'Listen, Sergiu said, moving in close and keeping his voice low. 'The only team you have is me. Anyone else is an outsider. People like us don't do teams. Understood?'

Dragos nodded his and kept schtum.

'Think before opening your mouth. Marius is here because he's a good cop and knows his way around murders. Right now we need him. But we have to make sure we'll get to whoever did this before he does, because that person will never go to trial. We cannot let people know about Silviu. The relationship with Marius is strictly need-to-know. He's a no fool and any extra information could put him on the wrong trail, and that would put his life in danger.'

'I know. I'll be careful. I'm sorry.'

'Enough. It's not that bad this time. But watch your mouth in future,' Sergiu said, his voice softer. 'Anyway, what's new?'

'Well, Raluca Demetrescu, Modrogan's fiancée, finally got back from Milan. She said the news of his death gave her such a shock that she's in hospital. I'll check. The thing is I called her and had a chat. Remember the jewellery Modrogan got from Gotica? It wasn't for her. Miss Demetrescu prefers gold, ideally with diamonds. It seems that Modrogan had one of the girls in his office send the silver to a certain address. Which she did, but then reported to Raluca. Apparently that's what caused the separate vacations. Guess where the pendant and the ring were sent to?'

Dragos paused for effect. Playing along, Sergiu rapped on the counter with his knuckles.

'The Dristor apartment. Modrogan put them in an envelope and wrote *for Amalia* on it. The secretary had one of the drivers deliver it.'

'Well done. Find out the secretary's and the driver's names. I want to talk to them.'

'I'll see to it in the morning. Do I tell Marius about this?'

'I'll do it. He won't come in tomorrow anyway. We're leaving for Voineasa on Monday. I told him to spend time with his wife, to enjoy the long weekend.'

'How nice of you.'

'It wasn't just that. I wanted a day to try and sort things out without him breathing on my neck.'

'I thought so.'

'Speaking of Marius. Did you do what he said? Did you trace the guy who delivered the food to Silviu's place that night?'

'I even talked to him. The man who ordered it paid cash and looked a lot like Silviu. The guy was half naked…'

Sergiu laughed. 'Good job, Dragos.'

'Was that a pat on the back? Wow … This calls for another beer.'

'I'll leave the celebration to you. I already have plans tonight,' Sergiu said, his eye on the shivering girl outside.

'What can I say? Have fun…'

'Dragos, don't be rude.'

Sergiu paid for the drinks, walked out of the door and walked up to the girl.

'Hello. What are you doing here?'

Taken by surprise, the girl dropped a handful of flyers that the rain quickly soaked.

'Working,' she muttered. 'As usual.'

'What sort of work is that? Looks like torture to me. You're blue with cold.'

The girl gave him a thin smile.

'I'm a waitress over there. It's quiet during the week, so we take turns in handing out flyers to try to get customers in. If I get ten then I'm free for the rest of the night.'

'And how many so far?'

'Three.'

'Good. Then we have only seven to go. Let's get them in then we can have a bite. How does that sound?'

Before she could reply, Sergiu took her by the hand and led towards the first gentleman he saw.

'Excuse me, I've invited this lovely lady to have dinner with me,' he said cordially to the bemused man. 'But she can't leave work unless she convinces ten people to have a drink in the Finnish club over there.

If you accept, you would be the fourth. Do you think you could help us out?'

The trick worked. In less than an hour there were ten new customers at the bar, commenting on the original publicity stunt.

'Now what?' the girl asked once her quota had been met.

'Well, I think we should introduce ourselves. I'm Sergiu.

'Alina,' she replied.

Sergiu elegantly kissed her right hand. 'Now tell me, where would you like to go for dinner?'

'Well, I don't know … I hear *Carul cu bere* on Stavropoleos Street is nice. I've never been there, though.'

'You've never been there?' Sergiu asked. 'The oldest restaurant in the city? Then we should go.'

The place was part of Bucharest's history, a landmark in the city. A few years back a restaurant chain had taken it over, but had maintained the traditional cuisine and look of the place. Even better, it was only a few blocks away. Sergiu took her hand and felt her shiver. He took of his jacket and placed it around Alina's shoulders.

'Be careful. It's heavy,' he said.

'What about you? It's a cold night.'

'Don't worry. I'll survive till we get there.'

The girl pulled the jacket around her and smiled gratefully. Sergiu put his arm around her as they walked.

*

Dragos got to work early. He assumed Sergiu would be late and since Marius wasn't coming at all it was better one of them was in, just in case. Sometimes Branescu would drop in unannounced to check up on them, something for which he had developed an irritating habit.

In any case, Dragos had plenty to be getting on with, not least brewing coffee and then placing the pastries he had brought with him on two plates. This need to keep everything nice and tidy was a habit he had picked up from his mother. He fetched Sergiu's ashtray, emptied and washed it, and put it back on his desk.

'I'm wasted on my day job,' he told himself. 'I would have made a perfect secretary.'

With the morning's rituals completed, he took one of the plates and sat at the computer, starting with the easy job. He had already picked a place in Voineasa for Sergiu and Marius to stay, a friendly B&B by the river where he and his friends had spent a weekend. He emailed the place to book two rooms and within half an hour the reservation had been confirmed. The first job of the day was done.

The harder prospect was finding a contact with the local police, someone smart enough to understand that his or her role would be to assist without asking too many questions. Diana in human resources had given him the names of five officers there, four men and a woman. Two of the men looked likely and were on the list of potential recruits. Dragos decided they were the safest options, but he liked the look of the woman who smiled at him from the ID photo on her file.

He was about to call the garage to get a car booked when his phone began to vibrate.

'Hi Sergiu.'

'Good morning. How are things?'

'Fine. I'm at the office, waiting for you to show up. I'm putting all the Voineasa stuff together for you and Marius.'

'Good. All quiet?'

'Peace and quiet.'

'OK. I'll be there in an hour and a half.'

'Sure.'

Dragos put down the phone and smiled. There was something reassuring about a call from Sergiu Manta.

*

Sergiu came out of the bathroom, went into the hall and gently slipped the phone into the inside pocket of his biker's jacket. Then went back into the bedroom and watched Alina sleeping for a while. The girl seemed lost in the white sheets. Her lips trembled slightly and a rebel lock of hair tickled her nose. Sergiu gently moved it aside. He realised he couldn't possibly stay in touch with her, but he was going to be a gentleman all the same.

He returned from the grocery store around the corner that he had spotted the night before with eggs, cheese, bread, tomatoes, ham, fresh orange juice, milk and coffee. When Alina finally woke up, she found Sergiu in the kitchen making an omelette.

'Hey, good morning. Sleep well?'

'Good morning. Fine. What are you doing?'

'Omelette for breakfast.'

'You're the first man who has made me breakfast.'

'In time one learns how to end a beautiful night. You know the definition of a perfect lover, don't you?'

'Go on. Tell me.'

'A man who makes love all night and turns into a

pizza in the morning. But you'll have to make do with an omelette.'

Alina laughed and blushed. They sat at the table and ate without speaking. The awkward moment came with the coffee.

'Will we see each other again?' Alina asked, already anticipating the answer.

'I get back to Timisoara today and…'

'…and you don't want to keep in touch,' she said, finishing his sentence for him.

'It's not that. I just don't know if there's much point. You're here, I'm on the other side of the country … But I'll email you.'

'No,' she said so firmly that Sergiu quickly looked up from his coffee cup and looked into her eyes. 'I don't want to write to you and end up waiting for an answer. It would be too weird for both of us.'

'You're right. It's better this way.'

They did the dishes together. Then Sergiu called a taxi. In the bathroom he used a napkin to retrieve from the bin under the sink the two condoms they used the night before, wrapping them and dropping them in his pocket. Coming out of the bathroom he found Alina in the hall, holding his jacket. Sergiu put it on then gave her a lingering kiss.

'If you ever come to Bucharest…' she said and Sergiu paused in the doorway. 'Then…look me up on Facebook and send me a private message. Alina Stanescu. It's a common name, but you'll recognise me from the profile picture.'

Sergiu sighed and kissed her on the forehead. She closed the door behind him as he left with a sigh that echoed his.

'That's the last I'll see of him,' she told herself in a low voice.

*

'Right first time, I want a Duster. I know they don't make convertibles in Mioveni. Yes, my friend, full option. And make it submersible, smartarse.'

Dragos threw the phone down on the desk, then looked up to see Sergiu.

'You're ruining my reputation, you know. The guys at the garage almost fainted when I told them what car I want.'

'Really sorry about your reputation, but going to a place like Voineasa in official capacity in the type of convertible rocket you like to use is out of the question,' Sergiu told him.

Dragos had a reply on the tip of his tongue, but the phone ringing put a stop to that.

'It's Marius,' he said, putting him on speaker so Sergiu could take part in the conversation. 'Hi. How's our super cop?'

'Fine. I've just been chilling with my wife and now she's resting. What about you guys?'

'Getting things ready for Voineasa.'

'Good. Have you spoken to the delivery guy?'

Dragos looked at Sergiu, indicating that this was his call.

'Yes,' Sergiu said. 'It looks like Silviu was the one who ordered and paid for the food. The delivery guy didn't see or hear anything out of the ordinary. But our victim was half undressed, which could mean…'

'That he was entertaining and had big plans for the night. I think our killer might be a woman. What do you say?'

'It's possible. And there's more. The zodiac jewellery that Modrogan bought from Gotica was sent to the apartment in Dristor, addressed to someone called Amalia.'

'Amalia Dresda,' Marius said. 'We really must find this woman and I hope we track her down in Voineasa. I'm almost envious of what you've achieved without me.'

'Don't be. You'll have your fair share to come, no worries.'

'That's not what I'm worried about.'

'Marius, what's on your mind?'

'Can I ask you a favour?'

'Sure.'

'Can you have someone watch my sister while we're away? Or, at least, monitor her phone.'

Sergiu raised an eyebrow.

'This isn't exactly legal.'

'Maybe not. But I don't want to ask my people in the police. I don't want them to know Alina is in trouble. Besides you guys seem to have the ability to operate more freely, from what I can tell.'

'Why? Is she in trouble?'

'She's acting weird,' Marius said. 'She's a waitress in a fancy club down in the city centre. She worked late shift last night and about 11 o'clock she texted the old lady to say she was sleeping over at a friend's place. Our mother wasn't that happy about it because she wanted her to clean up the rental apartment today. My parents own a small flat in the Berceni area and they rent it out. There's some theology student moving in there next week, so Alina was supposed to clean the place up and have it ready. I called her today around then and guess what? She was already there.'

'And isn't that good?'

'Look, every time my parents try to get her to do something she gets all fired up. But on the morning of her day off after a late shift she's already there at ten. Give me a break! I'll bet she spent the night there with a man. But at least I know it wasn't the jerk she's been seeing.'

'And you know that how?'

'Because he was picked up this morning, trying to steal a car.'

'Listen. Dragos will keep a discreet eye on her. OK?'

'I'll take care of it, Marius, don't worry,' Dragos assured him.

'Thanks. I owe you one.'

'Don't worry about it. See you later.'

Sergiu went out onto the terrace to have a smoke. Dragos followed him.

'You knew, right?'

'Knew what?'

'That the girl you picked up was Marius's sister.'

'In the morning, before I left, she told me her full name. I hoped it was a coincidence. It is a pretty common name.'

'Coincidence or not, now we have to manage this.'

'No. We don't,' Sergiu said.

That morning, when Alina told him her last name, Sergiu had felt a shiver run down his spine. The first thing that came to his mind was Alex, the boy from Brasov who recognised him during his first assignment for the Agency. Sergiu had managed to keep him away from that business. All the same, the Agency considered the boy too much of a security risk and put him away. Sergiu took that very hard.

'No?' Dragos asked.

'There's nothing for us to manage. Alina is a girl I spent the night with and she is well aware we aren't going to see each other again.'

'What if she tells Marius about it?'

'That's highly unlikely. And even if she does, there's no way she could tell him that the guy she spent the night with is me. A worst case scenario would mean that Marius wants to break my balls for screwing his sister.'

'I don't know, man. I don't like this.'

'Dragos, what do you want to do? If you tell Branescu, she's finished. And all for a one-night stand. Trust me, she's not a problem.'

Dragos spent a while thinking things over.

'OK. But if she becomes a problem, we'll have to take care of her.'

'If she becomes a problem, then we will,' Sergiu promised.

Dragos gave Sergiu a pat on the back and headed back to his desk. Sergiu got his black leather pouch and rolled a cigarette. He lit up and took a couple of deep puffs before crushing it out with a sigh.

*

Marius was sick of his cousin's bullshit. He was a mediocre reporter, but constantly bragging about something. He had never been overburdened with talent, but had been lucky. One winter a few years back he had been travelling somewhere near Calugareni in Giurgiu county, not far from where, four hundred years before, Mihai Viteazul and his men had vanquished an Ottoman army, against all the odds. Robert had been caught up in a heavy snowstorm on the road and shot footage of people and cars stuck in the snow. Then he had walked a few kilometres to the nearest house and got to use an internet connection to upload his material, rather than seek help for the stranded people he had just been filming.

That night a couple in their thirties died in their car and there were those who whispered that if Robert Anghelescu had been more interested in helping people than getting his material to TV newsrooms, that couple might still be alive today. All the same, the controversy gave him a reputation that boosted his career.

Marius watched his disreputable cousin working his charm on Meryem, and longed to get off the sofa and slap him. From the moment he had first met her, Robert had done his best to charm her. He told himself that it was as well that his wife was a smart woman who was not going to fall for it. Now he was showing her photos of his recent trip to Istanbul. Normally Marius would have stepped in a long time ago, but he knew his wife would enjoy seeing pictures from the city she had left when they got engaged, and which she had never set foot in since.

Marius felt responsible for the break-up between Meryem and her family. Although they had come across as modern, open-minded people, when the subject of marriage was raised, they had forced her to make a choice between her family and him. She made her choice without hesitation. Love gives you strength, he reflected, especially when you are young and idealistic. But now that she was pregnant, she wished she could share the happiness and fears with her parents. Meryem never complained, but Marius could sense how she felt.

Marius got to his feet.

'I'm just going to check your glory wall,' he said, referring to the section of the living room where Robert hung framed articles that he was particularly proud of. Marius always made a point of making fun of his cousin's pride in his journalistic achievements, and he knew the wall well already. He already knew the pieces on the Predeal sanatorium, the young gifted mathematicians, and the Braila theatre director who had finished up a beggar on the streets of Bucharest. Of course, the article about the winter tragedy in Guirgiu county occupied the centre. Then Marius noticed the most recent exhibit, an article about an IT specialist who had killed two people.

'This one's new,' he said, pointing at it.

'Not that new,' Robert replied. 'You haven't been here in a while. It's a story I did in Brasov.'

Marius looked carefully at the guy's photo. He was very tall, with long hair and a tee-shirt printed with a gothic logo. He took a closer look at the man's face.

'Fuck...' he murmured.

'Did you say something?' his cousin asked.

'No, not a thing.'

He didn't want Robert to imagine that any of his articles might have some real interest for him. He had no intention of giving his cousin that satisfaction.

But he made a mental note of the newspaper and the date it had been published. This was something he had to check it out, as he couldn't help noticing the resemblance between this IT killer and the super-agent he had been assigned to work with.

*

Sergiu gazed into the distance. he'd been lucky. The flat he was living in these days was on the seventh floor of a building behind the Titan commercial centre and had a magnificent view over the park. The sun was going down in a blaze of red that backlit a few thin clouds to create a sunset image ideal for any aspiring photographer. He took another gulp of beer and another drag of his cigarette.

In the living room Dragos was making fine adjustments to the stereo. He had come over to iron out the details and set up communication protocols. Their usual jobs were hush-hush and off the grid, while this time it was semi-official, with instructions and a clear paper trail. But even so, Sergiu was aware that once the murderer or murderers had been sighted, he would have to move quickly, before Marius could have any chance to take them into custody. Admittedly, he could finish off someone in jail as well, but that was more complicated. So that particular moment would require direct and instant communication with Dragos and the Agency.

So they set things up and now were able to take it easy. The speakers were grinding out something by Insane Clown Posse. Dragos grimaced as the song began.

'Touch my music and you're dead,' Sergiu told him.

'Wouldn't dream of it. Just turning it up so I can join you on the balcony.'

The music was loud and they could hear every word.

'Pretty weird, these guys,' Dragos said, pulling the ring on a can of beer.

Sergiu laughed. Then they sat in silence, admiring the sunset. Dragos broke the silence.

'Nice view. I think you're going to miss it,' he said and Sergiu gave him a hard look. 'C'mon! You've been staying here for six months already. You should have moved a long time ago.'

'I know,' Sergiu said with a sigh. 'I was hoping to stay a little longer. I like it here.'

'I know. That's why I haven't moved you on yet. Especially since you've been working outside the country. But now you're back home, and collaborating with outsiders as well. Once this job is done, you're out of here. It's for your own good. And Marius's,' he added with a meaningful glance. 'Not to mention his sister.'

Sergiu didn't answer. He knew Dragos was right. But the truth was that this everlasting state of limbo was getting to him. He dreamed of a steady place of his own, a few friends, a woman who would be by his side for more than a week. He was getting old. He glanced at Dragos out of the corner of his eye and wondered what the youngster's reaction would be if he were to ask him for help to disappear, to escape to somewhere beyond the Agency's reach. Would he help him, or would he sign his death warrant? They were partners and allies, they covered each other's backs, but what were the limits? How much of a friend was he?

'Sorry for ruining your evening.'

'No problem. It's a moment that has to come. Just find me somewhere nice.'

'Don't worry. You know I'm good'.

Sergiu nodded and took another sip. He sighed and wondered where he belonged.

*

Meryem waddled into the living room. She found her husband with his eyes glued to the laptop display, exactly where she had left him three hours before.

'What are you doing?'

'Research,' he said with an apologetic smile.

'It's two in the morning…'

'I know, sweetheart. I won't be long.'

'Come to bed soon, otherwise I can't get to sleep on my own.'

'Sure.'

Marius's attention was already back on his computer screen. Meryem turned in the doorway.

'You're not watching porn again, are you?'

He rolled his eyes in exasperation. A few years back an attempt to get romantic with his wife had been brusquely rejected, courtesy of migraine. She took herself off to bed while he had consoled himself with some entertainment on the internet. When Meryam woke and went to kitchen for a glass of water, she had found him engrossed in something that had shocked and angered her.

Marius struggled to understand why. It was not as if she'd found him in bed with another woman or something. It had taken a while to get back on good terms with her. But he learnt couple of lessons then. First, always make sure your wife has a bottle of water at her bedside. Secondly, small guilty pleasures are to be enjoyed on the mobile phone in a locked bathroom. Nevertheless, now and then, when Marius spent too much time on the computer, her suspicions would recur.

This time it was something else entirely. Cousin Robert's article had lodged in his mind. The guy in the picture had a long hair and a tee shirt with a gothic logo. But Marius could swear it was the same guy he knew under the name of Sergiu Petrescu. The man in the article was named Manta. He had been some sort of caretaker at a private military facility, until he killed the owner of the place and the retired officer who had helped run it. Marius continued to dig online and uncovered a lot more of the story than his cousin the journalist had managed to. This Sergiu Manta had been an orphan who had been fortunate to be adopted in his teens; something of a miracle and completely unexpected.

The boy's ambition and intelligence, coupled with his new family's support, lifted him from where he had been and turned him into an IT specialist; and a good one. He worked for a few years in the Philippines, where he met a girl and got married. But at some point he seemed to chuck it all away. He brought his wife and newborn son to Romania, settled them in Bucharest, and accepted a job at this military playground near Brasov. Nobody had been able to say for sure if this Sergiu Manta had known all along that the two managers at the camp were his uncle and his biological father, or if he picked that up after taking the job, but the end had been pretty bloody.

The murders were an act of rage. One of the local newspapers published an interview with a psychiatrist about the trauma provoked by life in an orphanage. Apparently the father and the uncle had abused the boy's mother, so he was the product of incest. The last piece of information about Manta was that he had died in Codlea prison following a fight. So it looked like case closed. And yet...?

This Manta character looked a lot like the agent Marius was working with. Even more, Sergiu the agent was also pretty smart with computers. Then there was the way he reacted when family connections were mentioned. And the tee-shirt in the picture? Marius was ready to bet that it was the type you could buy from the shop where the zodiac ring and pendant came from, Gotica. If he was right, and not just paranoid, this special B Company, that he had never heard of before, but which seemed to have unlimited resources, had staged the IT guy's death and brought him back to life with a new identity. The question was, why? What the hell were these people doing? And what about the dead agent? Was he a recycled ghost as well?

Marius set a reminder on his mobile phone. The next morning, before leaving for Voineasa, he was going to call Radu, a friend who was a prosecutor, and ask him to get the file on Manta's trial from the archives. The important thing was to keep his mouth shut and behave normally until he had more information. It was going to be pretty challenging; not just because Marius had always had a big mouth, but also because this homegrown James Bond was a very sharp observer.

He sighed and turned the laptop off. He had to get to bed before Meryam started fussing. Maybe he could even catch few hours of sleep.

*

'Fuck this,' Sergiu cursed as the freezing rain beat down, hammering hard enough on the roof of the car to make him shiver. He hated the cold, rain, snow and lousy winter weather in general. If this was how things were in Bucharest, then Voineasa was going to be much worse.

Going by the clock on the car's dashboard, Marius was late. They should have been on the road a quarter of an hour ago. He pulled his mobile from his pocket and keyed a text message.

C'mon, sweetheart, hurry up. I love you no matter what you look like.

He sent it to Marius's number and switched on the stereo, filling the car with a Finntroll's fusion of Viking and Irish sounds. He went back to his phone and this time opened the Facebook app. He didn't have an account of his own, but Dragos had set up and maintained a couple of dummy accounts for when they needed to use it. It was astonishing the amount of personal data that people seemed to be happy to share online. He keyed Alina Stanescu's name into the search box and immediately found himself looking into her blue eyes, with a lock of red hair over hair face. Alina's nose was wrinkled in a smile.

'What the fuck am I doing?' he muttered to himself, closed the app and shut down the phone before dropping it back into his pocket. As he did so, Marius's face appeared in the mirror, his hair awry and his clothes looking as if he had dressed in a hurry. He was clearly a bag of nerves. Sergiu got out of the car to help him with his luggage.

'Sorry. Meryam had morning sickness, and my sister didn't show up, obviously. She texted me she'll be along at noon. I don't know... She's my sister and I love her, but sometimes I could really kill her.'

'Is your wife better now?'

'Well, it looks like you have the chance to ask her in person. What the hell did I forget?'

Sergiu looked in the mirror and saw Mrs Stanescu approaching. The long white dress and the green coat on top of it complemented her dark complexion. Her black hair gracefully brushed her shoulders. Despite her visible pregnancy, Sergiu saw that she was stunning.

'You lunatic! If I didn't know better, I'd say you were in love,' she told him, handing him his service pistol.

'And you'd be right,' Marius said, gazing into her eyes. 'Oh, let me introduce you to Sergiu Petrescu, my partner in this investigation.'

'Meryam Stanescu, nice to meet you. My husband doesn't say much about you and that means he's impressed,' she said and presented a delicate hand with a pianist's long fingers.

Sergiu kissed her hand and smiled.

'On the other hand, I've heard a lot about you from your husband.'

'Don't believe everything he says,' she said. 'I'm glad he's not doing this trip on his own. It's good to know somebody's there to watch over him.'

'I won't let him out of my sight.'

'OK, I'll leave you to it. You've a long journey ahead of you. Drive safely.'

Meryam kissed Marius, and at that moment the phone in her pocket chimed.

'Your sister is on her way here,' she said, peering at the message. 'So don't worry, I won't be on my own.'

Marius kissed his wife on the forehead and watched until she was inside the building. He had no idea that she was walking back to their flat, wondering where she had seen this Sergiu guy before. There was something familiar about him.

In the car, Sergiu turned the music down as they set off. Marius closed his eyes. He was almost asleep when his phone rang.

'Hi there,' he said, answering the call, and listened. 'How's that possible? Well, thanks anyway. Keep in touch.'

'Trouble?' Sergiu asked, once the conversation was over.

'Just more bureaucracy,' Marius said. 'No big deal'

Sergiu nodded. He knew Marius was lying, and he had a gut feeling that this was something important. He made a mental note to have Dragos check the call.

*

Dragos took advantage of Sergiu's absence to put on something other than the usual heavy metal on the stereo. He made some coffee, his third cup of the day, and switched on the computer. He had to find a new place for Sergiu. This was one of the parts of the job that was always a chore, and the rule was that agents had to be moved at two or three-month intervals as part of the strategy of keeping their profiles low and the Agency secret. The problem was that these people eventually began to crave some permanence in their lives; a private place to grow accustomed to, to personalise, somewhere with a scratched wooden floor, a cracked window and a decent TV, a place with a dog and a few plants. They wanted homes.

He tried to compensate for this permanent state of limbo by finding places that would appeal to Sergiu. As he had come to know him better, he had come to appreciate his tastes and what he wanted from these temporary nesting places. Sergiu's current apartment had two big advantages; a view over the Alexandru Ioan Cuza park and the five islands dotted across its Titan Lake, and the proximity to the metro station. Sergiu liked to have something to watch unfolding before him, and the constantly changing life of the park acted like a screensaver for the mind. He also preferred to use public transport. He could have had a car from the Agency pool, but saw that as a liability, something that could be used to identify him.

During one of his night time walks through the city, Dragos discovered a building with apartments to rent. It was as central as it could get, on a small street near Romana Square. The next morning, he checked one of the apartments there. Two huge rooms, one of them semicircular, with a large crystal door between them, a typical pre-war place with high ceiling and tall windows. It was sparsely furnished, but what there was he could see was good quality. There were two balconies, and the one from the living room one didn't offer much of a view. In his contemplative moments, Sergiu would be able to watch a construction site, and considering the pace of work, it would look much the same by the time he had to move on. On the other hand, the kitchen had a smaller balcony overlooking an unkempt, overgrown inner courtyard. Dragos knew Sergiu would love this almost wild place. Now he was checking online to find out what the rent was likely to be, knowing that Branescu would not to be happy with it.

'How are you, Apostolescu? Everything in order? What are our boys doing?'

Dragos lifted his eyes from the computer. Where the hell had Branescu appeared from? He moved as silently as a ghost.

"They're fine. On the way. Left a bit late.'

'Why?'

'Something to do with Marius's wife. She's pregnant.'

'Well ... They'd better focus on the job, and be quick. You found accommodation for them? Do they have everything they need?'

'Of course.'

'OK. When you talk to Sergiu, tell him to watch his back. This morning a prosecutor named Radu Gresa asked to see his trial files.'

'What? Who the hell is Radu Gresa? And why's he interested in Sergiu?'

'That is what you're going to find out. Check this guy out and get back to me as soon as you find something. My guts tell me this Marius has something to do with it. Maybe this joint investigation wasn't my brightest idea,' Branescu said with a sigh.

Dragos didn't know what to say.

'All right,' Branescu said eventually. 'I'll leave you to it.'

He turned in the doorway.

'Dragos?'

'Yes?'

'This Gresa is top priority. I must know why is he digging into Sergiu's past.'

'Yes, sir.'

Dragos felt a shiver travel down his spine. Why would a prosecutor ask about Sergiu's trial?

*

"I've been told to assist you, and that you have complete freedom of movement. I don't know who the hell sent you, but you keep these people on their toes. In our defence, it's not every day that some big cheese born in Voineasa turns up dead in a hotel room in Sinaia. I presume that's what you're here for…'

The local police officer had a point. Voineasa had its beautiful river and stunning scenery, but was still a small mountain town where nothing much ever happened. Despite their best efforts, tourism hadn't really taken off. Few visitors came this far to enjoy the clean air and towering mountains, discouraged as they were by the lack of any decent roads. Nothing of any significance had ever happened up here and Modrogan's birthplace would probably have attracted even less attention if it hadn't been for his very public divorce and suspicious death.

'That too,' Marius answered cautiously.

Sergiu was discreetly studying Relu Dobre, their contact with the Voineasa authorities. He looked around forty, heavily built and with a shock of dark curly hair. He had obviously very recently become an ex-smoker as he constantly gnawed at the end of a pencil. He reminded Sergiu of a commercial promoting a toothpaste featuring the Mister Beaver cartoon character. This Mister Beaver, Dragos had told him, was a potential recruit for the Agency. They must have decided that the guy's capacity to talk had to be close to lethal, as he simply wouldn't stop.

'Most important, make sure you're dressed properly,' Relu said, glancing at Marius whose suede shoes had already lost the battle with the muddy streets. 'We have a bastard of a cold, muddy spring on our hands. May I suggest boots like his?'

He took the two Bucharest investigators into what passed for a meeting room. On the big round table was a tray with fresh coffee, water and cookies studded with raisins. 'Nice people,' Marius thought to himself, enthusiastically helping himself to one of the biscuits.

'Haven't tasted one of these since I was a kid,' he said.

'There's a bakery around the corner and they make great stuff. So, gentlemen, what do you need?'

'An office. This room's too big and you might need it. Access to your internet connection and to your database. Both computer files and archives. A landline – phone and fax,' Sergiu said.

'And we want to meet Modrogan's wife. As far as we know she's been living here since the divorce. Did you talk to her after the minister died?'

'No. Modrogan didn't die here. That was the Sinaia police's business and they didn't ask for any help from us.'

Marius nodded. The Sinaia force must have been off the case before they had a chance of investigating much.

'Ask your boss if he knows her. I think she should be officially informed of our visit.'

'Why? Are you frightened of knocking on her door?'

'It's not that. We'll be going there to ask some uncomfortable questions about her marriage, divorce, financial arrangements. I think it's best if we have the local authorities on our side.'

Sergiu was surprised by Marius' diplomacy.

'OK, I'll go sort all this out, before you get any more ideas,' Relu said, and was out of the door. Two seconds later he was back.

'It might sound weird, but I'm glad this murder brought you guys over here. Nothing ever happens in this place.'

'You're right, it does sound weird,' Sergiu agreed.

Relu grinned and was gone.

'So, we pay a visit to the lady of the manor?' Sergiu suggested.

'We have to start somewhere. They think we're here for Modrogan's death which happens to be true. It would be odd to start by asking questions about a poor forester's death. I don't think they need two cops from Bucharest for that one.'

Sergiu nodded. Marius was right, they had to start somewhere.

He felt his phone vibrating in his inner pocket. It was a message from Dragos.

Give me a buzz when alone. Must talk, he read

*

Mrs Modrogan – she had kept the name after the divorce – was an attractive woman in her mid-forties with waves of dark hair, brown eyes and small mouth with inviting lips. There was something of a Monica Belucci look about her, and she was fully aware of it. Relu had convinced his boss to call her and ask her to find time for the cops from Bucharest. The lady welcomed them with Turkish coffee and fruit.

From the moment they entered the house, the woman had her eyes on Sergiu. He fell back on the discreet smile that seemed to work every time, and he let Marius ask all the difficult questions. He intended to remain in the background when dealing with her. Although embarrassed, she provided what seemed to be honest answers. The motive for the divorce had been her husband's philandering. The latest escapade had been the final straw. This was Raluca Demetrescu, the blonde chief of staff the minister had become besotted with. He had thrown away a twenty-five year marriage for this woman. But, to be fair, he had been more than generous with the family's wealth. Daria Modrogan had come out of it with an apartment in Bucharest, the Voineasa home and a small place in the Austrian ski resort of Sölden. The name of the quiet town in the Ötztal valley caught Sergiu's attention.

'You're familiar with the resort, Mr Petrescu?' asked the former minister's wife.

'It's a rather exclusive one.'

'As I told you. My husband was very correct when it came to money. More than that, he took it upon himself to support me. So, you see, I had every reason to wish him well. Now I'll have to think up some sort of business. Or even worse, get a job,' she said with a smile, as if she had just told a joke.

'Mrs Modrogan, think back to the seventeenth of March. Where were you? Please take us through the day,' Marius said.

'The day my husband died,' she said with a sigh. 'I assumed you would ask that and it's been on my mind. I'm afraid there's not much to tell. I was here. Since the divorce I rarely leave Voineasa. I spent a week in Sölden in January, but apart from that ... Anyway, as I said, I was in town. Did some shopping before lunch; cheese, fruit, coffee, that kind of thing. I brought everything home then I went for lunch at the Blue Poplar.'

'Blue Poplar?'

It's a pub at the edge of town. It's not great. In fact, it's pretty lousy, but the owner and I have been friends since we were children. At night it fills up with drunks and deadbeats, but at lunchtime it's quiet. We get together, have a bite to eat, talk. His name is Stefan Gruia. He can confirm I was there.'

'No doubt he can,' Marius said drily.

'Then I went home,' she said, continuing without seeming to notice his remark.

'What time did you get home?'

'Around five in the afternoon. My housekeeper was on her way out and she always finishes by five.'

'All right. We'll have to talk to her as well.'

'I'll get her to the police station tomorrow morning before work. Is that all right?'

'Yes. That'll do for now. We won't keep you any longer.'

The two men stood up to leave. Sergiu kissed her hand and she smiled. In the doorway, Sergiu turned to face her.

'Mrs Modrogan, I'm sincerely sorry for your loss. It is obvious that in spite of the divorce you were still fond of your husband.'

'Thank you, Mr Petrescu,' said Daria.

Once they were in the car Sergiu rolled a cigarette and lit up.

'Did you just remove Daria from the suspect list?' asked Marius.

'Not necessarily. But a little diplomacy could come in handy, as you said. And the fact that she still loved her former husband doesn't mean she wasn't capable of killing him. Women are strange creatures.'

'Tell me about it!'

'On the other hand, if we're looking for a serial killer, she doesn't really fit.'

'That's true. So, what do we do? Go to that Poplar place?'

'I think we should go in the morning. Waving some police ID and asking awkward questions in a pub full of drunks isn't the smartest idea.'

'But is it wise to give the lady time to fix her alibi?'

'If there's something to be fixed I think she did it already. Besides I'm tired out and I'd like to get to the hotel and get a bite to eat. And, more importantly, something to drink.'

'A beer would go down well.'

'Or a whisky. Or palinca if they have any.'

Sergiu finished his cigarette and threw the butt away. They got into the car and he drove away fast.

'Is someone thirsty?' Marius said.

*

If there ever had to be a prototype of a classical housekeeper, Fanica Manea would definitely have been the one. She was a rotund lady with curly hair, dyed in a deep, unnatural shade of red, and she wore round glasses. Her blue floral print dress struggled not to give way to the pressure. Her hands, red from the chemicals she used every day, rested in her lap. She tried to stay serious, but her eyes glowed with excitement. No doubt her involvement in the inquiry would be the highlight of the day in her building. She was rather disappointed that the only thing they asked of her was to confirm her employer's arrival time on the seventeenth of March. But, as someone said once, never let the truth get in the way of a good story. So that was advice she followed as Fanica's fifteen minutes of fame stretched to twenty and beyond.

Sergiu indulged her enthusiasm. This was most likely the most exciting thing to happen to her in years. It crossed his mind that he would probably never get to her age – and maybe that was not necessarily a bad thing.

Daria Modrogan smoked as she waited for her housekeeper, standing by her dark blue Jaguar. Sergiu remembered an article about the late minister. They had a picture of him smiling, leaning against the same car. So the wife had got to keep that as well. The man had indeed been a gentleman.

'So? Did Fanica cover for me? Or should I give her the car keys and get ready for handcuffs?'

'Ma'am, please!' Fanica said, but Sergiu and Daria ignored her.

'I can't reveal any elements of the pending investigation.' he smiled.

Daria laughed. Fanica got in the car, after lingering for few seconds, looking into Sergiu's eyes.

'Are you going to the Blue Poplar today?' Daria asked as she got behind the wheel.

'Did they announce it on Facebook or something?'

'No. I spoke to Stefan this morning. Be patient with him. He's not the friendliest person in town, but he does know everything around here.'

The Jag left a lot of smoke hanging in the air as she drove away.

On the stairs at the entrance of the building, he found Marius smoking.

'Making new friends?' he asked.

'More like acquaintances. Hurry up with that smoke. We need to get to that bar before our visit becomes public knowledge. The way news is spreading around here, I think we'll have a welcoming committee.'

*

Sergiu took a critical look at his partner's outfit.

'What? Are you shocked?'

'Well, yes, that's one way of putting it…'

A laughing skull was stretched over Marius' belly.

'Isn't it funny?'

'Yes it is, but it's not really you.'

'Why? Wearing skulls on t-shirts is only for metalheads?'

'No, but … well, I didn't expect it and I was surprised, that's all.'

'Aren't we all full of surprises?'

Sergiu didn't answer but was aware of the hidden meaning. Dragos had told him Marius had been digging into his past. He even had a prosecutor check the files on his double murder trial. It wasn't ideal either for Marius, or for the prosecutor, especially since Branescu had got wind of it. Sergiu would have to talk to Marius when this was all done. But not now. The cop could hardly keep his mouth shut and it was most likely he would let something slip. It was important to find out how much Marius knew, and where his information had come from.

But now they had other priorities to focus on. Stefan Gruia at the Blue Poplar would most likely back up Daria's story, but Sergiu and Marius were hoping to get something useful out of him. If the man was as up-to-date with local gossip as she had said, then maybe he could help in establishing a link between victims. Most likely the forester was involved at a certain point with the old lady in Dristor and they had a child who was now out of reach. But what was the connection with Modrogan and Silviu? And why were all these people dead?

Sergiu was caught up in his own thoughts, when Marius's voice brought him back in the real world.

'Hey, you missed it.'

'What?'

'The Blue Poplar. It was that red brick building.'

'Red? That's way I drove past it. For fuck's sake, it ought to be painted blue.'

*

The bar owner had the look of Kenny Rogers fallen on hard times, and as expected, he confirmed Daria Modrogan's alibi. He was a withdrawn character, but all the same, it wasn't hard to see that he harboured a fondness for the lady in question. That must have suited Daria just fine, Marius decided. Any lovelorn heart needs to find comfort somewhere.

The real nugget of information was dropped in at the end of the conversation.

'Modrogan wasn't a bad guy, God rest his soul,' Stefan Gruia said. 'But he couldn't keep it in his trousers. He hurt Daria badly and, in the end that destroyed their marriage. And it almost got her in trouble with that zodiac woman.'

'Come again?'

'There's a girl about the same age as my son. Maybe a bit older. Must be around thirty. She comes from an old line of crazy fortune teller women. They have some intuition that's inherited from one generation to the next. They also knew how to use local gossip, so the word got out that they were good at it. One of them, the great-grandmother of this one, knew a thing or two about herbs and added a witchcraft flavour to it. And it worked. People can get taken in by a lot of shit. Well, thing is those women were never lucky in love. Or didn't want to get into it, God knows. This last one I'm talking about is just gorgeous, and smart with it. If she'd had any kind of an education she could have gone a long way. But even so, she learned a bit of astrology and became good at it. She even worked with some glossy magazines. And she had her way with guys. None of them could resist. She left my boy a wreck. I don't think he's over yet.'

'So she's quite something?'

'And how. For the life of me, I can't see where she

gets it from. That mother of hers, Elena Dresda, and that drunken guy were hardly anything to look at.'

Sergiu and Marius both started as the name was mentioned, but didn't show it.

'Dresda?'

'Yes, that was the girl's name.'

CHAPTER FOUR

Sergiu leaned against the leather sofa and closed his eyes. After talking to Stefan Gruia, the two of them sought refuge in a coffee bar to try and make sense of what they had heard. Marius's intuition was proved right. The old lady in the Dristor district had been involved with the first victim, the forester. According to the bar owner they were never married but they had a daughter. Amalia had used her mother's Dresda family name.

These Dresda women had been running a fine business in fortune telling for generations. No matter what they called themselves – witch, healer, fortune teller or astrologer – they succeeded in convincing people to pay for good gossip combined with female intuition and some shrewd deduction. Stefan Gruia was right; despite the economic and social progress, people still chose to believe in this kind of nonsense, Sergiu reflected.

The most important piece of information concerned Amalia Dresda. Marius had been right; the girl was a suspect, to say at least, and now they had more questions than answers. How and when had she and her mother made the move from Voineasa to Bucharest? How come there was practically nothing on record about the pair of them? How had Amalia become involved with Modrogan? How was Silviu got mixed up in all this? Was she the woman the agent had spent his last evening with? And the big question: why did so many people around this girl end up dead?

'At least now we have reason to dig into the forester's death,' Marius said.

'You think so? There's no proof he was Amalia's father.'

'No. But everybody says so. According to Gruia it was common knowledge. And it's a good enough reason to look at the files.'

'Maybe,' Sergiu replied. 'Although I'm not sure it would be much help. It seems the father didn't really keep in touch with either the woman or the daughter.'

'Well, he knew enough to get killed. If we're right about this, he was the first victim.'

'And that's a big if. You realise his death might have nothing to do with anything. It's very different to the others.'

'Could be,' Marius admitted. 'But I doubt it. That would be too much of a coincidence. Hopefully the circumstances of his death could lead to some information about the girl.'

'Flat chance. I doubt anyone looked too closely into his death.'

'Probably not. But now we have to try. We don't have much on this girl, and we simply can't pin her down.'

'You should pay another visit to your friend Daria,' Marius said, turning to face Sergiu. 'If Gruia was aware of Modrogan's affair with Amalia, then she must have been as well, and didn't bother to tell us. Maybe she would be more open if it's just the two of you.'

Sergiu smiled.

'All right. But I'd like to have a word with Gruia's son first. If I'm to ask her personal questions, I'd like to know a bit more first.'

Marius watched as Sergiu took the black leather pouch from the pocket of his camouflage trousers and rolled a cigarette.

'Filthy,' he muttered as Sergiu licked the cigarette paper.

'Why? My licking, my smoking. If I let you lick it, that would be filthy.'

*

Relu Dobre, the local police officer assisting the pair from Bucharest, gasped with astonishment.

'What file was that?'

'The guy who died in the woods', Marius repeated, enjoying the look on the man's face.

'Wasn't that an accident?'

'I don't know,' Sergiu broke in. 'Was it?'

'Even if it was an accidental death, you still must have a file on it. We're not interested in his death. But it might help us with some information on a person of interest to our case.'

This wasn't entirely true, but Marius and Sergiu had no intention of making the mistake of letting the local police think they were checking on their work.

'What person on interest?'

'Amalia Dresda, his daughter.'

'That crazy fortune teller? I'm not that sure she's his daughter. I mean he said so, but the guy was as ugly as hell, God rest his soul. And the girl is really stunning.'

'You know her?'

'Yes. I arrested her the day Modrogan's engagement was announced in the press. The woman got wasted, got to Daria's home and started throwing stones at windows. Mrs. Modrogan called 112 and we had to pick her up. She was howling that the minister was her man.'

'Can you show me the incident report?' Marius asked.

Relu looked uneasy and started fussing. Marius raised his eyebrow. Sergiu smiled.

'Who said old-fashioned chivalry is dead? Nothing's further from the truth. Our boy here didn't want Amalia to have a criminal record in addition to a broken heart.'

Dobre flushed and looked at his shoes.

'Her story about the affair with the minister was bullshit. I mean she was a looker, but even so. Modrogan had Daria, and the blonde tart in Bucharest. But even though she was hysterical and in tears, I couldn't book her,' he said touching his chest.

'So you ignored all the rules,' Marius muttered.

'Don't be such a jobsworth,' Sergiu told him. 'The man has a sensitive heart. She threw some stones at the windows. What's the big deal?'

'The big deal is that she would have been easier to track down,' Marius replied.

'How was I to know?' Dobre asked.

'Right. Marius, how could he have known?' Sergiu grinned.

Marius was so furious that Sergiu's teasing went over his head and he slammed the door on the way out.

'Next time, do bear in mind that the heart is on the other side.'

'I keep forgetting,' Dobre said. 'Is he really angry?'

'Marius? He'll get over it. Let's have a coffee.'

'Good idea. We'll go to the place across the street, so we can smoke as well.'

'You smoke?'

'If you'll roll one for me,' Dobre replied with a smile.

'I'll roll you one. But don't expect any hippie dreams. It's just straight tobacco.'

*

His mother told him that before the Revolution, people believed that the secret police, Securitate, had tapped everyone's phone and read every letter. That was practically impossible. It would have required thousands of listening devices and an army of agents. But the terror was so widespread that people took this urban myth for granted.

Now, in the era of electronic mail, smartphones and social media, bugging phone conversations had become a joke. In the nineties there had been a street rumour that Russian smugglers could provide a radio receiver that allowed you to listen to mobiles within a certain range. Dragos Apostolescu was fascinated by the way these wild tales would find their way into the public consciousness. The technical means were there, but as the volume of communication grew at an ever-increasing rate, the problem was the same as back in the old days of landlines and letters; the lack of time and human resources. But the smart IT people had come up with a solution, programming monitoring systems to search for certain keywords in mails and conversations.

Dragos's job description, if there had been one, also consisted of monitoring the communications of a few people connected to Sergiu Manta's former life – his ex-wife, his son, his foster parents and a few others. That morning the system signalled that there were a few emails containing some key words Dragos had previously set. The messages were sent and received by Camelia, a woman with whom Sergiu had shared a brief but intense relationship when he embraced his new life. Dragos opened the mails in question.

He swore the moment he moment he realised the subject of the messages. When he was recruited, Sergiu had been assigned a code name, as any reports on agents' activities referred to them strictly by these code names. Sergiu had once owned a dog named Arkon, which was where his code name had been drawn from, and Arkon was one of the preset trigger words. This time the dog was the subject of the emails, and the news wasn't good.

Dragos was still trying to decide whether to call Sergiu or wait until he came back, when the system delivered another alert, and this time the message had nothing to do with an elderly German shepherd.

*

It's not easy for someone who has never had a dog to understand how close the bond can be. Many pet owners see themselves as parents and treat the animal like family. More than that, they talk to the animal and identify human characteristics in their pet's behaviour. Which is, of course, completely wrong.

The relationship between Sergiu Manta and Arkon the German shepherd was nothing like that. Sergiu had been quiet and introverted to begin with. All he required from his dog was to be a ... dog. Arkon accompanied him everywhere in that army camp. Their private time together consisted of Sergiu sitting on the porch of his wooden cabin with a beer in one hand, the other one scratching the dog's head. Sergiu thought about how scared the poor dog must had been when their ways had parted. Sergiu had killed two men and was on his way to prison. Arkon ended up with one of the few real friends Sergiu had ever had. Cristian Herra, the military police officer who tried to prove Sergiu's innocence, against all odds. When he finally understood that his friend was the murderer, Cristian had to choose between career and friendship. They had met during the course of the investigation but it felt like they had been friends for ever. He risked both his career and his friendship with his partner, Andrei Cruceanu, in order to give Sergiu the opportunity to escape. Sergiu often wondered what if? What if he could have taken his wife and child and run for it? Cristian Herra would still be alive, that's for sure. Sergiu suddenly realised that death had been a part of his life long before he ever heard of Branescu and the Agency. He smiled sadly.

Dragos had found out that Radu Gresa, the prosecutor Marius had asked to check on Manta's trial, was asking questions about the missing file, and that was not good. On the one hand, his life as an agent required complete secrecy. On the other hand, all this fuss was very inconvenient for a few guys with a lot of power and no sense of humour.

That raised another question for Sergiu. Was Silviu's death part of the series of murders that had ended with Modrogan's killing? What if his colleague's assassin merely figured out he could link this killing to the other murders? They still had no proof of a connection between Silviu and Amalia Dresda, the girl they couldn't track down. The only thing they knew for sure was that Silviu spent his last night alive with a woman, but nobody had ever seen her, plus they also had that bizarre drawing resembling the zodiac jewellery – but that could have been planted in Silviu's house after the murder.

A loud knock on the door made Sergiu jump.

'Hey, are you OK?' Marius asked.

'I'm fine.'

'Good. Let's make a move, then. The bar owner called. His son showed up. He's waiting for us.'

'Coming...' Manta said, washing hands.

*

Sergiu hadn't seen one of these old Russian Ij motorcycles in years. His instructor back when he was getting his licence had one. They weren't exactly friends, but had a special relationship based on their shared passion for bikes. Sergiu had spent a lot of weekends in the old guy's garage helping with bike maintenance and acquiring some basic knowledge of mechanics. So Sergiu was surprised to find that the pub owner's son, Rares, owned one.

He and Marius hoped the boy could help them find Amalia. It was pretty frustrating that in the era of Facebook and Twitter, the woman had managed to remain off-grid. She had no property of her own, no job, no credit card, no phone number and she obviously no longer lived at her legal address. According to some people she would show up in town now and then, staying just long enough to stir up trouble. It was clear that she had been involved with one of the victims – Modrogan the minister.

The talk of the town was that she was the forester's daughter. There was nothing on her on any database, so they had no idea what she looked like. Dragos had commissioned a portrait artist in the Agency to produce a present-day likeness based on the childhood photo they found in her mother' home, which gave them a fairly vague sketch. The artist argued that the picture was not very sharp and the subject had been photographed from a distance, so the facial characteristics were far from clear. As a result, the likeness they had to work with could easily belong to a quarter of the female population of the country.

'It looks like we're back to good old-fashioned police work,' Marius sighed.

Rares Gruia looked to be in his mid-twenties, Marius guessed, maybe a bit older, but not more than thirty. He was tall and thin, with big, blue eyes set in a bony face, that waged a constant battle with its bad skin, and topped with a mop of fair hair. Sergiu wondered where the hell Gruia had been when the kid was conceived, as there was no resemblance whatsoever.

Talking to the police made the boy visibly nervous. He continually fussed over the bike without doing anything in particular. Sergiu took a look around the spacious, well-organised garage. There was plenty of equipment in there, some new, but much of it quite old, which told him that Rares was not the first owner of the garage – or of the bike. He couldn't help noticing a laptop and some testing gadgets. These were of no use for maintaining the antique Ij, so Rares had to be taking care of other people's wheels as well.

Marius, on the other hand, examined the relaxation end of the garage, fitted with a small refrigerator, a TV and a stereo, old but good quality.

'Well, well, isn't this a real man's cave?'

The boy nodded.

'Both the garage and the motorcycle belonged to my grandfather. If it isn't all leather and show, my father is not interested.'

'At least your grandfather made a living for himself with these toys. For you this is all a hobby. You start things but never finish anything. You abandoned those photography courses, after buying that expensive camera. You took courses in mechanics, but never graduated. At least you didn't spend any money on the garage and the motorcycle. You inherited them,' Gruia said from the doorway. It seemed that an invisible barrier prevented him from entering.

'I make my own money, one way or the other. I never came begging to you,' the son retorted.

'Not that I'd ever give you any.'

'Mr Gruia, we appreciate your putting us in touch with your son, but it would be appreciated if we could now have a word with him in private,' Marius said. 'This is confidential and we really need this information.'

The old man backed off with bad grace.

'When you're done, come over to the house to have a coffee ... or something stronger,' he said and glared at his son. 'If you can restrain yourself from saying anything stupid, you can come to dinner. I'm cooking,' he said as a parting shot.

Sergiu watched him walk away. He no longer seemed as confident and full of himself as he'd been at their previous meeting. Once he was left alone with Marius and Rares, Sergiu turned to the boy.

'Let that bike be, you're not doing any work on it. Let's talk about Amalia.'

*

Stefan Gruia ambled home wrapped in thought. When Modrogan had divorced Daria he thought he had hit the jackpot. He had been besotted with that woman since childhood, but he'd always considered her way out of his league. He had grown to accept that he was always going to be just a friend. But when her husband started to develop an eye for younger women, he thought this could be his chance. For a heartbroken Daria he would be the supportive knight in shining armour. But then Modrogan died and he soon realised that competing with a ghost was no easy matter.

It's funny, he thought, but when it comes to the dead, people remember only the good things. Who would have thought that Daria could forget all the tears she'd shed because of that shit of a husband of hers? Just because the idiot had met his death in a hotel room in Sinaia, where he had no business being in the first place! Complete bullshit! On top of all that, this Sergiu shows up from nowhere. He was that type of man, half-savage and half-gentleman, that Daria could not resist being drawn to. With Modrogan out of the way, Gruia had allowed himself to consider Daria his woman. Now he had to deal with this punk from Bucharest.

As if that wasn't enough, those cops were interested in the relationship between his son and that crazy bitch Amalia. Gruia felt like slapping himself for having told them about that. It was obvious from their reaction they had no idea. That fool Rares would do anything to protect the girl and that would get him into trouble, sure as anything. The kid couldn't cope with pressure and Gruia was concerned he would do something stupid.

He still had nightmares about the depression and the drug addiction his son had gone through when Amalia and her mother had moved to Bucharest. Then the girl started showing up now and again, and Rares did nothing but wait for her. When she was around, he became her perfect and devoted slave.

Overwhelmed by his guilt and self-reproach, Gruia reached home without realising it. His hand went into the pocket for the keys, and the first thing he felt was the mobile phone. The cool feel of the metallic case made him smile. That cool smartphone was a gift from his Daria … Daria! He quickly dialled.

'Daria, dear, hello, it's me. Sweetheart, I think I put my foot in it when I had that chat with those cops today…'

*

The waitress smiled patiently. Marius was trying to sweet-talk her and failing utterly. He was drunk, but determined to prove that he was a man of style, which apparently included reciting some classical poetry that he could hardly remember. Thank God the girl had a sense of humour.

'C'mon, Sergiu, help me out. I can't remember the damn poem.'

'My friend, my knowledge of poetry is strictly limited to rock ballads.'

'Good! Sing one!'

'Marius, let the poor woman be! You've been torturing her long enough.'

'Torture? Have I done that, miss? If so, please acc … accept my apo … apologies…'

Marius collapsed into a chair next to Sergiu.

'Aren't you something else … married man and all,' Sergiu asked with a smile.

Before Marius could come up with a reply, Sergiu felt his phone vibrate. Picked it up and read the message.

'Well, well…'

'Well, what?'

Sergiu handed him the phone.

'Of course,' Marius complained. 'I'm breaking my balls here trying to impress a woman, and all you have to do is smile to get them to fall into your lap.'

'I'm not so sure.'

'What do you mean?'

'Marius, we're old enough not to fall for this. A woman like that does not throw herself in the arms of a newcomer like that unless…'

'Unless she needs to fool him.'

*

The sun was bright and sparkled on the water. The landscape was simply stunning, but the chill morning air made Daria shiver. She was waiting for a signal from Sergiu. To place his coat around her shoulders, or his arms around her. Something. Anything. What was wrong with this guy? Was he gay? Impotent? Shy? Or maybe ... No, no way. She wasn't in her twenties any more, that was true, but she still had it. She knew that. She saw it every day in the eyes of the men crossing her path. She saw it in Stefan's eyes; especially in his eyes. Normally she wouldn't have even looked at him, let alone let him come close. But after the divorce she had been vulnerable and alone. She had needed someone who would worship her like a goddess. Stefan Gruia had always been hopelessly in love with her, had always placed her on some sort of pedestal. Now that her life was back on track, Daria felt it would be unkind to simply shake him off.

But then this Sergiu Manta showed up, a man with an easy, natural charm and bursting with masculinity. He came across as silent and impenetrable, and when he smiled, she felt that old fluttering in her stomach. The woman in her couldn't resist temptation on this scale.

But Daria had a second reason for trying so hard to please the newcomer. She had a few secrets of her own that were now bubbling up dangerously close to the surface. Daria hoped she could convince Sergiu to let them stay out of sight.

Her train of thought was interrupted by Sergiu's embrace. He glanced at her breasts, their plump roundness bringing a smile to those impassive lips. Her nipples had hardened in the cold breeze.

'Cold?' he whispered softly.

'It took you forever to notice.'

'I noticed a while ago, but I wasn't sure if I should…'

'You were wondering whether to let a woman catch cold or not?'

Sergiu turned Daria around and looked into her eyes.

'Not just a woman, this woman. I know you're playing games. So tell me, what are we really doing here? And skip the admiring the landscape bit, if you don't mind.'

*

Marius threw away the cigarette before entering the bar. Once inside, he bought another a pack. He was nervous and the investigation centred around this girl was dragging on, a girl nobody seemed to know anything substantial about. The simplest, most obvious theory was that this girl killed them all. But instinct told him it had to be more complicated than that. And there was also the boy, Gruia's son, who was defending Amalia Dresda like a dog guarding its backyard. He wasn't too smart, but he had strength. It was possible that he and the girl had committed the murders together, especially if she had a talent for playing the victim.

On the other hand, there was the question of motives. If Amalia really did all of them, alone or helped by the biker boy with the bad skin, the question was why? Modrogan seducing and abandoning her, breaking her heart, was understandable. But that poor guy posing as her father? Or her mother? And what about the super agent's colleague?

Had Amalia been the girl he had invited over? Or was this just another lousy coincidence? The problem was that if the murders were not connected, he was in deep shit. On the other hand, if he was right about all that – and so far it seemed that he was – than he had to deal with this special agent, and he had reason to believe there would be consequences. All this secrecy around the mysterious Agency could hardly be good news. The fact that the trial files on the murders committed by Sergiu Manta – the likely real identity of his new partner – were missing from the archives was at the very least suspicious.

As if that was not enough, he was now having to deal with his wife's jealousy over the phone. For some reason, she seemed certain he was screwing every woman in Voineasa. As if, he reflected bitterly. His single clumsy effort to hit on one of the local women had been an epic failure. In fact, he was so embarrassed about it that when Relu suggested going out for a beer, he avoided meeting him at the hotel's bar. They chose the Blue Poplar instead.

He placed his hand on the bar doorknob and instantly felt something sticky. He needed to tell Voineasa's answer to Kenny Rogers that there were plenty of cleaning products on the market.

'Hello,' Relu, said, greeting him with a big smile. 'I thought you got lost or something.'

Marius wondered what this smartarse was so cheerful about.

*

Sergiu slipped off the bed. He couldn't sleep and he was starting to feel hungry. From the bedroom door he turned back and gazed at Daria for a while as she slept. One of the scented candles on the bedside table still burned brightly, bathing her body in delicate golden light. The angelic face with those lips that demanded to be kissed was surrounded by a flood of dark curls. A tiny dimple on her forehead, right above the nose, gave her a slightly melancholy look. He took in her delicate neck, firm breasts, neat waistline, the swelling curve of her hips and long legs. Sergiu smiled and left the room.

Daria was a beautiful woman and time had been kind to her. Her husband may have tired of her charms, but she would have no trouble finding some decent man. Instead, she had apparently chosen to bury herself in this Godforsaken dump with that joke of a bar owner. He had no doubt that those two were a couple.

She had tried to explain why she hadn't mentioned her husband's affair with Amalia Dresda from the outset. She told Sergiu that she had been suspicious of that strange girl who had shown up on her doorstep one day and frightened her. Amalia had found out about Modrogan's forthcoming marriage from the papers and she'd become a human tornado; screaming, kicking, throwing stones at windows. Daria tried to calm her down and told her that he was no longer living there. But the girl was so enraged that it was impossible to get through to her. Daria had been deeply disturbed by the depth of her anger. When a stone whizzed past and missed her by inches, she decided it was time to call the police. Later, she decided not to press charges. She had felt sorry for Amalia. Stefan Gruia had said it was beneath her to fight with such a crazy child and he succeeded in convincing her.

Sergiu wondered why Gruia had taken Amalia's part in this. The girl had been cheating on his son with the former minister, or so people said. At any rate,

Amalia was in love with this man, while the Gruia boy yearned for her. It was all too complicated…

Sergiu's thoughts were interrupted by Daria's arms snaking around him.

'I like the way you smell. What are you doing here? I woke up in an empty bed and thought you'd gone.'

'I remembered the strawberries and cream. Want some?' Sergiu asked, opening the fridge.

She took a strawberry, dipped it in cream and giggled as she reached out to put a fingerful on his nose.

'I'll get you for that!'

She laughed as he loped after her, a grin on his face, and cornered her between the table and the window. Glancing over her shoulder, he thought he caught a glimpse of movement outside in the darkness by the fence. He paused, peering through the window, but the darkness outside and the light behind him obscured his view and all he could see was his own reflection in the glass.

Daria had her arms around his neck and pulled him to her.

'I don't know what you're looking at, but I won't let you ignore me for one second…'

'Is that so?'

He stretched his arms around her, hands on her buttocks as he pulled her close, bit her ear, and kissed her passionately. Her fingernails softly grazed his back. Sergiu felt himself getting hard. He lifted her onto the table and his hands roamed her body. Daria moaned softly. She returned his kisses, then gently pushed him away and dropped her head to begin exploring his body with her lips, working gradually downwards until she knelt in front of him. Sergiu's breath came in gasps and he leaned back, his eyes closed.

Beyond the window the soft clicks of the camera's shutter were lost in the sounds of the night.

*

The phone bleeped and a red light flashed. Dragos hoped it wasn't another love message from Angela. All her sweet talk was going to give him diabetes. He stretched for the phone.

'What the fuck?' he muttered as the lamp on the table clattered to the floor. He had forgotten that it had been plugged in to charge.

The message wasn't from his girlfriend. It was from Sergiu, and as always, it was brief and to the point

Daria Modrogan. Where does the money come from? Dig deep.

Goodbye lazy evening, Dragos sighed and got himself off the sofa. His first port of call was the fridge to put a couple of pastries on a plate. He closed the fridge, thought for a moment and opened it again. He added another two pastries to the plate and put one in his mouth to chew while the coffee machine produced the large latte he had asked for.

He put the plate and the cup on a tray, added a glass of lemonade and took everything into the living room. Dragos closed his laptop on the desk and switched on the big desktop computer. This time he needed some heavy weaponry. There was work to be done...

*

Sergiu lit a cigarette and took his time to watch the sun rise before getting into the car. Daria had wanted to know why he was in such a hurry to return to the hotel and he replied that it would be better for her reputation if he wasn't in the house when the cleaning lady showed up. In addition, he would also find himself in trouble if anyone were to find out that he had become involved with someone who was part of an ongoing investigation. He chose his words carefully, stressing the involvement, which mollified her.

'Besides,' he said, turning it into a joke, 'I have to act like a good lover. You know what a good lover does in the morning?'

'No.'

'Gets dressed and goes home.'

Daria laughed, kissing him goodbye.

Sergiu left in a buoyant mood. He had spent a wonderful night, but he was aware that he needed to lose the smile from his face before encountering Marius. The insistent buzzing of his mobile brought him back down to earth.

'Are you alone?' Dragos asked and Sergiu could hear the excitement in his voice.

'I am now. You were very close to interrupting a special moment.'

'Aren't you supposed to be at work? I spent half the night digging up information while you…'

'Same here, but different methods. Do I detect a note of envy?'

'No comment… Anyway, back to business. I think I've opened the Pandora's box.'

'And what came out of it?'

'All sorts of bits and pieces…'

*

'My friend, you never cease to amaze me.'

There was no irony in Marius's voice. He hadn't expected to find Sergiu having breakfast in the hotel's restaurant after his night with Daria Modrogan.

'Good morning!' Sergiu smiled.

'Good morning to you too. How was your night?'

'Really, Marius?'

'Yes, I know, a gentleman doesn't kiss and tell. Never mind, I have a lot to tell you. Unlike other people who were out having fun, some of us were hard at work gathering information,' Marius said.

'You too?' Sergiu thought. 'I must have missed a real big news night.'

CHAPTER FIVE

'And he just told you that son of his isn't his after all? Just like that?' Sergiu said in surprise, placing his laptop on the table.

'Well, not quite.' Marius thoughtfully chewed a pretzel. 'At first he greeted me and Relu like old friends. Then he asked about you. I said you had some work to do. Relu made a stupid joke about you being some sort of night hunter and winked. Gruia must have suspected something about you and his girl. He was drinking pretty heavily. You know he usually doesn't say much. But now we couldn't stop him even if we wanted to. He said a lot of shit like women being bitches and love being a curse, that kind of stuff. But he also said one or two interesting things.'

'Like what?'

'The story goes like this – he and Daria grew up together. It seems the big house had belonged to her grandfather, so the dead minister wasn't that generous after all. Anyway, those two met each summer, when the princess visited her grandparents. When they became old enough for things to get dangerous, Daria's father stepped in. Gruia was just a mechanic's son. So the lord of the manor made him a once-in-a-lifetime offer. He stayed away from the girl and, in return, the old man fixed him a job on a merchant ship.'

'No shit…'

'It looks that way. For three years our bar owner works hard and makes some money, some smuggling as well, I'd guess, as I can't see how he could make that sort of money honestly. When he came back he had enough money to buy the bar. The only problem was that he found Daria hooked up with Modrogan. She wasn't interested in him any more. He had a few affairs, then he met the girl he married. Everybody thought it was a big romance. In fact, she had been raped and was pregnant. He said he took pity on her. Can you believe it?'

Sergiu scratched his head through his buzzcut hair.

'Can you?'

'Not really. I mean it sounds like a script for a rom-com. But we can check a few facts; him being in the merchant marine, the marriage, his son's birthday. It is true that all these happened after the '89 Revolution, when everything was complete chaos, but still ... Maybe you can ask Dragos to do some research?'

'I will. But even if the story checks out, what can this possibly have to do with our murders?'

'The only death that fits is Modrogan's.'

'Can you see our bar owner waiting twenty-five years for revenge? And just at the very moment the Modrogans were getting divorced? I don't think so.'

Marius paced the room, lost in thought. Suddenly he stopped and turned toward Sergiu.

'What if we're looking at it from the wrong angle?'

'Meaning?'

'The only motive we took into consideration is connected with these people's private lives; love, hate, relationships between parents and children. But I find it hard to believe that a few failed romances could cause so many deaths. What if there's more to it?'

Sergiu looked at the policeman without answering. Then he opened his laptop and hid behind it.

*

Daria flinched when she saw Sergiu sitting on her porch, smoking. She took the shopping bags out of the car. He took them from her wordlessly. She smiled but got a hard stare in return.

'So you're not here because you missed me?'

'We have to talk. And it's not going to be pretty.'

In the kitchen. Sergiu placed the bags on the table and the housekeeper quickly took them from him. Daria gestured to Sergiu to follow her into the living room.

'What do you want to talk about?'

'You lied to us,' Sergiu said with a sigh.

'Me?' Her surprise was unconvincing. 'When?'

'The whole time. You led us to believe that your former husband was generous with you over the divorce. But he was fair at best. Your family was the one with the money, not him. This house belonged to your grandfather. He managed to save it somehow from being confiscated by the communists. Obviously, your family integrated into the new social order, since your father, son of a bourgeois landowner, managed to get a high ranking job at Dunarea. And we all know what they did, running trade and channelling the proceeds to the secret police to run their agents abroad.'

'You say it like he was an operative for the 5th Directorate of the Securitate before their place was burned down in the revolution. He was an economist, for God's sake!'

Sergiu scowled. He knew that the Dunarea Company had controlled all of Romania's overseas trade during the communist era. Officially, it had been the intermediary between Romanian producers and their partners from other countries when in fact it had been a cover for intelligence operations and part of the Foreign Information Centre. Not all its employees had been secret police officers, but every single one of them had been checked by the Securitate and they had to deliver periodic reports as part of their job. Sergiu knew that some of Dunarea's former staff had seamlessly morphed into the new intelligence structures. The chickens and their shit were coming home to roost.

'Yes, all right. My family did make some compromises in order to keep our privileges. They weren't the only ones who turned themselves into communists after the war. And who can blame us? There were people who died in prison waiting for the Americans to come. And my husband *was* generous...

'How so?'

Daria sat down on the chair by the piano, her hands on her lap. Sunshine coming through a gap in the curtains lit up her face. All of a sudden, Daria Modrogan looked her age. Not any wrinkles, as her complexion was immaculate, but her eyes. They had that sad, weary expression of someone who has carried a burden for far too long.

'I met Gruia during a summer vacation. We started

dating. Dad didn't like it much, but he thought it was just going to last one summer and then it would be over. To his surprise, when I started my first year at university, I was still his girlfriend. We wrote each other when apart, and when I was here we were inseparable. Until one day my father introduced Sebastian Modrogan to me. He said he was his young colleague. It worked much better than expected. I was smitten then and there. All of a sudden I understood what my father meant when he said I deserved much better than Gruia. Although now I'm deeply ashamed of that.'

'Why? Just because you and Gruia are together now?'

'Gruia and I are not…'

'Daria, please … Don't take me for a fool. You shouldn't be embarrassed you are a couple. There's nothing wrong with that.'

'Oh, I see. I'm an old, abandoned woman and therefore…?'

'It has nothing to do with that. You have a broken heart. We all need someone to love us when we're down.'

Daria looked hard at Sergiu, but he avoided catching her eye.

'Aren't you an understanding man? It doesn't seem

to bother you to be involved with some other man's woman. Or maybe it's not the case? Maybe I'm just a one-night stand for you.'

Sergiu reached out and gently held her chin, making her look into his eyes.

'Sweetheart, I didn't expect any of this to happen. And I'm not the kind to wham-bam-thank-you-ma'am. But I came here to do my job and when that job is done I'll be gone. I'm not delighted with this situation, but I don't want to mess up whatever you have with Gruia. I don't want you to be left alone when I'm gone.'

Daria's eyes filled with tears, so Sergiu pulled her into his arms and hugged her.

'The truth is I can't manage on my own. I've always been a bit of an airhead. I suppose that's why my father put everything we had in Sebastian's name once we got married. So, you see, he was more than fair at the divorce. He owned practically everything.'

For a while they hugged in silence. Sergiu was the first to speak.

'Daria, you must understand something. I was sent here to investigate your husband's murder. Next time I ask you something, please don't lie to me. It only makes things more complicated.'

She nodded and said nothing. Sergiu gave her a kiss and turned to leave.

'You know, I think Gruia is a decent guy and really cares about you,' he said from the doorway. 'But if you are not happy with this relationship, you don't have to put up with it. And that thing about being an airhead? I don't think so.'

Daria stood in the centre of the room for a long while after he had gone. Then she shook herself and went to the kitchen.

*

'Care to share your whereabouts, sir?' Marius said as Sergiu appeared.

'Daria's. To get a few facts straight.'

'And did you?'

'Yes. What have you been up to?'

'Picked up my mail. And it's damn interesting, too,' he said, handing him a heavy yellow envelope.

Sergiu looked at it on both sides.

'No written address. How did you know it was meant for you?'

'It was on the bed in my hotel room.'

'I see… May I?'

'By all means.'

Sergiu opened the envelope and scanned the photos. He examined them carefully, one by one, while sensing Marius anticipating his reaction. He knew the moment when these were taken, just as he and Daria had been downstairs, naked, sharing strawberries in her kitchen. The photographer must have been hidden behind the fence.

'We need to find Gruia's boy.'

'Why?'

'He has a passion for photography, and he owns professional cameras. These were taken at night, through the window, from a distance. You need more than a smartphone or a cheap camera for that. And we still can't find the mysterious Amalia and this is starting to get on my tits. Something tells me she's involved in all of this.'

'One thing's for sure,' Marius said taking the photos from him. 'The camera loves the pair of you.'

He smiled and a second later he was doubled up with a well-placed punch to the stomach.

'What the hell's got into you?' he said, struggling to get his breath back.

'Next time keep your thoughts to yourself,' Sergiu snarled.

Marius struggled to stand upright again. He made a mental note that his partner was a sensitive type and jokes might not always be appreciated.

*

Branescu entered the office. This time there was nothing silent about him and he appeared to be in a hurry.

'Sorry to interrupt. We have an emergency,' he said shortly.

'No problem,' Dragos replied, looking up at his boss eagerly, like a puppy hoping for a reward. Branescu handed him a flash drive.

'You have some documents and some mail drafts on this. This has to find its way to the media. Email addresses,' he said, handing him a scrap of paper.

Dragos nodded, eyes wide.

'And it has to look like an anonymous source from inside the prosecutor's office,' he added.

'And how are we going to do that?'

'Look it up. Find someone over there with a grudge against this Gresa. Than invent a mail address on a public server and send the information to the addresses I gave you. Do it so a basic investigation would lead to Gresa's disgruntled colleague.'

'What if the patsy takes action on this?'

'Dragos, if it was just about creating a fake email address and sending some information, you wouldn't be in the picture. Do something with those IPs. Make sure you cover our backs. If you have to, break into the guy's home and send the email from his computer. But do pick someone competent.'

Dragos looked into Branescu's eyes for few seconds, as if to make sure of what he was being told to do. Then he took the flash drive and the note.

'Fine. No problem,' he said plugging it into his laptop.

The boss spun on his heel and left without another word. Dragos opened the files and read through them. He stared at the screen and whistled. He looked through the list of names and searched them out on his database.

Things were about to get tough for Prosecutor Radu Gresa.

*

Sergiu waited for Rares to show up at the garage. He waited until the youngster unlocked the door, and stepped in behind him. Before the boy could figure out what was happening, he was pinned against the wall with Sergiu's hand firmly on his neck.

'You like playing with the grownups, shithead?'

'I don't know what…'

'Don't give me that. What did you think those photos would get you? Did your old man have you keeping an eye on his girlfriend, or did your precious Amalia put you up to it?'

'Take your hands off me!'

'When you start talking. Or when I feel your neck breaking. Your choice.'

'Can't do that. You're a policeman.'

'We're investigating a state official's death. You have no idea how much freedom the right victim can give us.'

'You're bullshitting me.'

'Maybe I am. But do you have the balls to risk it? I didn't think so! So, start talking. Why did you take the pictures and where's Amalia?'

The boy wriggled Sergiu's hand free of his throat. He let him catch his breath.

'I swear I don't know where she is. Somewhere around here. When she needs something, she calls. Last night she texted and said she needed my camera. I didn't ask why. I never ask anything,' he said morosely.

'Where did you meet?'

'Behind my father's bar. That cop, Relu, and your partner were in there.'

Sergiu couldn't help thinking about Marius's face when he would hear that he had been literally steps away from that girl. He could hardly wait to tell him. After apologising for punching him, of course.

'And you really didn't ask her where she lived, what trouble she was in?'

'No. I tried that once and she threatened never to speak to me again. And I believed she had it in her. I can't risk that, you understand?'

Sergiu nodded. Despair was a universal language, no matter what caused it.

'I asked if she was all right, if she needed anything. She told me not to worry. She was fine, she has her little place in the woods.'

'Little place in the woods?'

'A joke of ours. Amalia said that if she was Little Red Riding Hood she would find a decent wolf and a little place in the woods and forget all about the grandmother.'

Sergiu sighed.

'Look. Amalia is in deep shit. She's a suspect in Modrogan's murder. The longer she hides, the deeper she sinks. And she's pulling you down with her.'

'She didn't kill anybody. I'm sure of it.'

'For your sake, I hope you're right. But she definitely knows something about this murder. Make her show her face. Otherwise you'll be the fall guy and I don't think you want that.'

Rares looked down in silence and Sergiu began to feel sorry for him. He didn't enjoy coming down hard on the boy, but there was no choice. He was about to leave when a thought struck him.

'When you talk to her, tell her that her mother was murdered. Maybe she'll be interested.'

The boy looked at Sergiu with big round eyes. He silently congratulated himself that his hunch had been right. The boy knew nothing of the old lady's death. And, most likely, Amalia had no idea either.

He left the garage and got into the Duster where Marius smoked as he waited.

'Did it work?'

'I think so. I'll tell Relu to have the boy followed discretely and get Dragos to monitor his phone.'

*

'Weird,' Sergiu growled, looking at his computer's display.

'What?'

'Dragos did some digging into Amalia's finances. It seemed she had a notary taking care of the paperwork. According to the documents, Miss Dresda purchased the apartment in Bucharest before selling the house in Voineasa. Where did she get the money from?'

'Maybe she borrowed and returned it after selling here…'

'Look at this! You know who bought Amalia's house? Our very bar owner Stefan Gruia. He knocked the place down and built the Blue Poplar. It looks legitimate; the man spends his years at sea, makes some money, buys an old house, opens a bar. Amalia sells a house and buys a flat in Bucharest. All too clean to be true.'

'Yeah, Marius said and stretched. 'Or maybe we're paranoid and we see secrets, conspiracy and cover-ups everywhere.'

'Maybe, but I doubt it. If everything really is out in the open, why didn't Gruia mention buying the house from Amalia?'

Marius went to the window and glanced outside. The sky wasn't overcast, but it was sodden grey. You could feel the pressure of the approaching rain. He turned to his partner.

'You said Daria's father was with that secret police company, Dunarea. He worked with Modrogan. And he was the one who arranged a job on a merchant ship for Gruia. All these things happened shortly after the revolution and a system like that doesn't really die. Is Amalia part of the gang too?'

'It doesn't really fit.'

'But what if it's just a front? Some sort of cover?'

'A cover for what? We have no proof of any shady business.'

'But we can't track her down. And it's not like we are some sort of amateurs here.'

'True,' Sergiu admitted.

'If you ask me, the girl is hiding. If she's simply a fortune teller, why does she try so hard? And how come she's so good at it?'

*

Sergiu opened the window and took the rubber mat from his travelling backpack. He stripped down to a pair of sport shorts and started out with some light stretches. He had neglected his fitness since they had arrived in Voineasa and he felt stiff. Every stretch made his joints crack.

'I can't afford to be lazy,' he told himself. 'At my age it's not easy to stay in shape.'

From the warm-up he moved on to increasingly complex exercises. The autumn wind coming through the window helped. He was doing push-ups when he heard a sharp beep. He got to his feet and went to the chair where he had hung his biker jacket. From the inner pocket he got the old mobile he used to communicate with Dragos. The message was brief – *Watch the news!*

He took a long sip from the water bottle by the bed and started looking for the TV remote, eventually finding it by a bedside table. He scrolled through three cartoon channels, four shopping channels, three movie and two porn channels before he finally got to the news.

For a few moments he wondered why Dragos would want him to watch something about football, before he thought about reading the news briefs scrolling past underneath. The yellow headline was a bad weather warning for the southern half of the country. The red one displayed breaking news about the arrest of Bucharest prosecutor Radu Gresa, accused of beating a suspect during an interrogation.

Sergiu tried another news channel and then another. It looked like sports reports were being broadcast on all of them simultaneously, so he had to wait ten minutes to get a full report. The story was that three years previously Gresa had been in charge of a rape investigation in which the victim had been a teenage girl. The prime suspect was a career criminal with a long history of violence against women. Caught up in the nightmare of establishing proof, the prosecutor had become closely involved in the case. The allegation was that, since the evidence was circumstantial, things had got rough and ended badly when Gresa tried to extract a confession.

Not only did the suspect refuse to make a confession, he and the victim subsequently got married, leading to the charge being dropped. Three years later the former suspect produced affidavits stating that the violence during investigation had impaired the use of his right hand. Once things had been set in motion, other testimonies about the prosecutor's violent outbursts surfaced. Journalists found an ex-wife who said that, although her husband never abused her, he had always had a fiery temper. Although this was hardly enough evidence for a court case, there was no doubt that Gresa's career was over.

Sergiu knew exactly what had triggered this. Gresa had been set for a fall from the moment Marius had asked him to check the Manta files. In a way, the policeman's friend had been fortunate, as others who became a nuisance to the Agency ended up much worse than this. In this case, the tactics had been to give the target something else to keep him busy. However, Sergiu was sure that it wouldn't take Marius long to join up the dots and their working relationship was likely to become more challenging.

'Fuck this shit,' Sergiu growled to himself, realising that he would have to open up to Marius – and he didn't relish the idea at all.

He was still pondering this when the door crashed open and slammed all the way back to the wall. Marius was in the doorway, his face red with fury and his eyes ablaze.

'Just who the fuck are you, Sergiu MANTA? And what's so fucking important about this Agency of yours that people have to suffer so your friends can remain hidden?'

*

Sergiu was alone in the lobby bar. None of the staff were there at this hour of the night, but he poured himself a whisky. In fact, he took a glass and the bottle and set himself to drink. With every sip he took, his swollen lip hurt. He ran his tongue over it and it stung even more.

He could have beaten the hell out of the policeman the moment he banged open the door, but Sergiu wanted to give him the opportunity to burn off some of his anger. He let Marius throw a few punches before twisting him into the wall.

'Get out of my room,' Sergiu hissed into his ear. 'Otherwise I'm going to beat the life out of you and drop what's left into a hole in this Godforsaken dump. I swear you won't live to see that child.'

He was convincing enough for Marius to leave without a word. There was no way he could sleep after that, so he came down to the bar to try and relax. He was deeply frustrated about the situation he'd been dropped in. He'd known from the outset that it would pan out like this. Marius was a determined policeman who would stick with his investigation. Worse still, he was a good, decent guy.

A lifetime ago, when he graduated from high school and had no intention of pursuing any further studies, Sergiu had been called up for his compulsory military service. As a youngster with a big mouth, he very quickly fell foul of authority and ended up serving his army time in Vanju Mare, a run-down military base in Mehedinti County. Back then the military service had been a farce. The food was bad, the hygiene poor, the rules just plain stupid, and the backwater of Vanju Mare was worse than most.

Sergiu discovered there what pure stupidity really meant. He still felt anger blaze inside him as he remembered the routine humiliations, the long hours of training on Sin Hill with the burnt tree at its peak. The story was that during a storm a man sought shelter under it. The tree was struck by lightning and the man died. Old women whispered that the poor man had lived sinfully and had been punished by God. So they called it Sin Hill.

That arsehole of a sergeant had made them run with gas masks on all the way up to the burnt tree. Naturally, none of the recruits could make it to the top. But the torture wouldn't stop until every one of them was spitting blood into his mask. When one of the youngsters ended up in hospital, Sergiu took it into his head to give the sergeant the beating he so richly deserved. Without a word to anyone, one night, when the NCOs were drinking together, Sergiu sneaked out of his barrack room and kept watch. More than an hour passed before the sergeant came out to relieve himself. Sergiu could still see him in his mind's eye; a short, stocky man with a cigarette in the corner of his mouth, swaying on his feet. That was the moment Sergiu chose for his attack. And he'd have been successful if it hadn't been for Vasile.

He was a boy from the mountains around Sibiu, a shepherd. He hadn't cared much for school, but he had a quick mind and a keen sense of humour, so he and Sergiu quickly became close. Vasile understood him and kept an eye on his friend. Just as Sergiu was about to make his move, Vasile jumped on his back, dropped a bag over his head, knocked him unconscious and dragged him back to the barracks. If it hadn't been for this man, Sergiu would have probably killed the sergeant and ended up in prison. Thanks to Vasile, he survived his military service, got his act together, went back to school and built himself a career in IT.

Marius reminded him of Vasile.

Sergiu sighed, laid his head on the bar and closed his eyes. The creak of the door startled him. Marius was standing in the doorway. Sergiu stretched over the counter, took another glass, filled it and showed it to the cop. Marius nodded, walked slowly to the bar, dropped himself into a chair with a grimace of pain on his face, and took the glass from him. He emptied it and, without a word, held it out to be refilled.

'Now talk,' Marius said to Sergiu.

*

'Honestly, there's no woman, Mer, I swear. If I wanted something to fuck, I wouldn't take the trouble to go all the way to the middle of nowhere. No, I've no intention of cheating on you and I'm not trying to prove a point. Is that clear?'

Meryem's jealous outbursts were no fun. In fact, Sergiu would have considered them annoying if he had time to care. But his mind was elsewhere.

They had spent the previous night drinking and talking, Marius and him. Sergiu had told him a thing or two about himself and the Agency. The policeman's arrogant cousin had been among the journalists covering the two murders he had committed and his trial. Sergiu was forced to admit that his real name was Manta.

He'd also filled Marius in about his background. His birth mother, Corina, had discovered in her teens that her mother's husband was not her natural father. She was the result of an affair her mother had once had with a very powerful man who had no intention of abandoning his wife and two sons for Corina's mother. Although he never bothered to legalise the situation, he established a relationship with his illegitimate daughter as she grew up, and Corina became close with one of her half-brothers and his best friend. Those two took advantage of the girl's innocence and longing to find a family, and forced her into a brutal, humiliating and incestuous threesome. Corina died in childbirth and Sergiu was sent to the orphanage for fourteen years of torment, loneliness and bullying. he'd been fortunate to be adopted in his teens, but, in some ways, it was already too late by then.

'And the wife and kid?'

'I met her when I was working in Asia in IT. It was...'

'...love at first sight?'

'No. That's not my style. But I liked her. She was petite, delicate and naïve. And as sexy as hell. She brought out the best and the worst in me. But something made me hesitate. I had no intention of moving there and I wasn't planning to fall in love or anything. But I finally took her out and one thing led to another. You get the idea.'

'And you married her.'

'Well, it's a bit more complicated than that, but yes.'

'Have you ever regretted it?'

'Me? No. But I think she did.'

'Why? I think there are plenty of girls who would like to have you in their lives.'

'That's because they have no idea what they'd be getting themselves into. I'm fun for a crazy affair, but I'm not husband material. And then I was sent to prison and left her behind with a child to raise…'

'You abandoned her the moment you killed those two, not when you were sent to prison.'

Sergiu smiled.

'That's a cop speaking.'

'No, I mean it. Did you have to do it?'

'Have you ever been in an orphanage?'

'No.'

'Well, I spent my entire childhood there. That's where I learned how to be brutal. That's supposed to be the most formative time of our lives. And when I looked into my origins, I discovered I was the son of a tormented teenage girl and the scumbag was my uncle. I don't know how to explain this, but those two were entirely evil. They had to be wiped out.'

Marius was silent for a while.

'And your wife and child?'

'They're fine. They think I'm dead. It's better this way. I keep an eye on them from a distance.'

Sergiu chose not to mention that one of the first things he did on joining the Agency was to ensure that his former wife's abusive boyfriend disappeared.

'You know,' Marius said. 'This is my worst nightmare. That if something should happen to me, Meryem and the child would be alone. Her parents cut her off when we got married and…'

'Maybe you should try to talk to them?'

'Me? They don't answer Meryem when she calls. What makes you think they'd talk to me?'

'They wouldn't, probably. But if you send them a message telling them they're about to become grandparents, I doubt they would just ignore it,' Sergiu said and Marius scowled back at him. 'You've got nothing to lose, if you ask me. They don't like you anyway. Worst case scenario? They won't reply. But at least you tried.'

'And what the hell am I supposed to tell them?'

'I don't know. That they are to have a grandson or a granddaughter and that you want the child to have grandparents, that it's important for the new arrival to stay in touch with his or her Turkish heritage. Look, a child can sense when things are not right in the family. It's good to have someone to turn to in time of need. You'll be a father. Maybe you should put aside your ego for a while.'

'Is that what you did?'

'Sort of...'

All of a sudden the door slammed against the wall as Relu rushed in.

'She's been spotted!'

'Who?'

'The fortune teller, of course. One of my sources...'

'Where?' Marius asked.

'An alley by the Blue Poplar.'

Without a word, Marius and Sergiu grabbed their coats and hurried out to the car.

'Hey, wait for me!' Relu cried, rushing to keep up.

CHAPTER SIX

Sergiu and Marius were like chalk and cheese. In spite his physique and skills in close-quarters combat, Sergiu disliked unnecessary violence. He was calm and introverted. Women certainly liked him, but he was incapable of maintaining a long-term relationship. Maybe he simply didn't want to. Marius, by way of contrast, had a big mouth, was untidy and distracted. He loved his wife dearly even though he moaned about her, and his past wasn't as juicy as he made out.

But the two had much in common. They were both intuitive, quick thinkers and natural investigators. And they discovered they were also good watchdogs, as they sat in the car staking out the street behind the Blue Poplar where Amalia had been last seen. They hoped that Relu's source hadn't sent them on a wild goose chase. They had the local police checking every house on the street. There was a slim chance she might be hiding out in one of them, although she could easily slip away through a back door or a window. But what was the alternative, just sit there and hope she would show up?

The crime movie cliché of two partners having deep, meaningful conversations during this kind of operation occurred to Marius. In real life, of course, it was very different. The two of them were too focused on not missing any movement to spend time exchanging confidences.

Sergiu suddenly looked up, alert.

'Seen something?' Marius asked.

'Don't know. I thought I saw something. There, by the house with the red door.'

Both of them peered into the darkness, but everything appeared to be still. Still, if Sergiu was certain that he had seen something. Marius trusted his partner's instinct, if nothing else about him. The guy was all secrets and that Agency of his was deeply suspect, to say the least, but Sergiu had a good nose and sharp eyes.

'What do you think...'

'Down!" Sergiu shouted before Marius could finish his question.

The two men flung open the car doors and hit the pavement at the same moment, just as the bullet punched through the windscreen in front of them.

'Fuck me…' Marius breathed, getting to his feet and drawing his service pistol. It took him a while to notice that Sergiu was standing still and gazing at a fixed point fifty metres from their position.

'I saw her,' Sergiu said, answering the unspoken question.

'What? Who?'

'Amalia. She was there, by the pillar.'

'Damn it, man! Why didn't you run for her? Or shoot?'

'In mid-town, with people all around us? What were the odds? She was there for a second then she was gone.'

'Shit! Shit! Shit!'

*

Sergiu lay in an armchair, head back and his eyes closed. His right hand cradled a whisky glass. Daria caressed his forehead and arms with an ice cube, her gentle movements accompanied by kisses.

'Are you angry with me?' she whispered.

'Why should I be?'

'For showing up at the police station. But I heard you were shot at. You didn't answer your phone and I was terrified.'

'Sorry. In all the confusion, I left my phone in the car. I was going to call you anyway.'

'But would you have come if I hadn't kidnapped you?'

Sergiu smiled, took her by the hand and gently pulled her into his lap.

'Kidnapped? And how hard was it? Did I resist?'

Daria giggled and kissed his neck.

'I'm glad you came. I left at the right time. Marius was fighting to keep me from beating the hell out of your chief of police. And he was on the verge of losing it.'

'You don't like the local police?'

'It's the chief I don't like,' Sergiu said. 'He's out of his depth with this whole thing and he won't admit it. He sent his men to track Amalia down.'

'And that's bad?'

'It's the best way to help her escape. That girl is really good at staying under the radar. She's going to make fools out of them and we'll waste precious time.'

'Maybe they'll get her,' Daria said

'Not a chance. They don't know what they're up against.'

'And you do?'

'Well, I know she's not a poor fortune teller. She just pretends.'

'Why? What's she hiding?'

Sergiu shook his head and didn't reply.

'I have the feeling you know more then you're telling me,' Daria said.

'Leave the investigation to the professionals, and stick to what you do best.'

'Which is?'

'Taking care of this man you kidnapped,' he smiled, his hand slipping between her legs.

'I'll do that, but first there's something you need to know about Amalia. Fanica, my housekeeper told me. I was going to call you, but the shooting happened and...'

And what?'

'Did you ask for the file on Vasile Petrache's death?'

'Even Fanica knows I asked for the forester's file? What is this?'

'It's a bit more complicated. The police archivist lives in Fanica's building. And over there, everybody knows...'

'Knows what?'

'Fanica and Vasile were lovers, before Amalia's mother lured him away from her. She says they were engaged. She was really hurt when they split.'

'Well, if he wasn't a Casanova...'

'Laugh all you like, but he wasn't always the poor old bastard you might have heard about.'

'I know that. I found a photo from his younger days.'

'Well, then. Anyway, finding out that you're investigating his death again shook her so badly she couldn't even work. She was a mess, so I made her sit down, opened a box of chocolates, poured a drink and made her tell me the whole story. I admit I don't always take much notice of her stories, but this time she said something interesting.'

'What?'

'She said Petrache couldn't be Amalia's father. The man fired blanks, if you get my meaning.'

'Really?'

'That's right. She wanted kids, so they went to the doctor who checked them both out. Fanica says she has proof.'

'You're right, that's interesting. I'll have to talk to her. But for now you ought to take care of this poor man who almost came to a bad end today,' Sergiu said with a sly smile on his face and his hand inside Daria's blouse.

*

He could remember every single moment. The dog had stood still, his eyes nearly popping out of his head, as if unable to believe what was happening. Sergiu had dropped to one knee and spread his arms wide. The dog finally decided to trust his memory, bounded over and hurled himself into the man's embrace. He trembled, whining as he licked Sergiu's face and hands, unable to show the full extent of his happiness.

But it was all over now. Sergiu had only just processed the news from Dragos that Arkon had died. It had been ages since They'd last seen each other, but he felt the loss of the animal deeply, thinking back to the last time he had been able to hold him in his arms. Sometimes he wished he was able to shed tears, but he had long since lost that ability. In any case, even if he could, he wouldn't do it in front of Marius.

Suddenly, the policeman's voice pulled him out of his thoughts.

'Who would have thought that a crazy girl could be quite so dangerous?'

Sergiu turned and looked at Marius, who was gazing out of the window. Sergiu knew he wasn't looking at anything in particular. He was just trying to cover his fear. The adrenaline effect had passed now and emotion had taken over.

'Is this the first time you've been shot at?'

'Yeah,' Marius said. 'I usually make my appearance when people are already dead. Investigations aren't anything like as slick and smart as American cop shows make out.'

'No job ever is. Sometimes I wonder if Hollywood isn't just a big recruitment agency.'

Marius was tempted to ask Sergiu if his work was anything like fiction, but decided to keep quiet.

'Anyway, I don't think we were in any real danger.'

Marius raised a questioning eyebrow. Sergiu rose and picked up a photo of the car's windscreen taken by local forensics.

'Look at the entry point,' Sergiu said, a finger on the photo. 'Right in the middle, where the rear view mirror is. The only chance my head or yours was going to be there was if one of us was putting on lipstick. And since there wasn't much danger of that... Anyway, if she'd wanted to kill us, we'd be dead. She's anything but a crazy kid.'

Marius frowned but didn't say anything.

'We'll get her in the end, won't we?' he said at last.

'Sure. I'm not leaving until we find her.'

'And what if she did kill all those people? What happens then?'

'I report it to my boss.'

'And then?'

'Then I follow orders.'

'And what if you won't like the orders?'

'We are talking about a twenty-something woman suspected of four killings. One of the victims is a colleague of mine. Is there anything about this I'm supposed to like?'

'It's so much easier when you are involved with a secret agency, isn't it? You get an order, you follow it. No questions asked. Not even to yourself,' Marius said, and could sense Sergiu's growing irritation.

'First of all, we haven't got Amalia yet. I've made no report, and neither have you, because there's nothing to report. When the time comes, I have no idea what my orders will look like. But somehow you seem to know better?'

Marius stepped closer to Sergiu and leaned over his desk.

'Get this into your head. I'm not going to allow you and your gang to trash someone's civil rights, regardless of what that person is accused of. Is that clear?'

The two men glared at each for a moment. Then the policeman stalked out of the room, slamming the door behind him. Sergiu sighed and turned his attention back to the display on his desk.

*

Fanica was on her way to work. She was anxious to get there and talk to her boss, but she was also apprehensive. The curly-haired, chubby policeman had told her the detectives from Bucharest wished to speak to her. The first time she'd been required to answer questions, it had made her feel important. she'd simply been asked to corroborate some facts concerning Daria, and there was no uncomfortable detail that she'd been asked to reveal.

Now this was something else entirely. These guys were digging into her life, into her very soul. The curly-haired boy had told her they were interested in her life with Vasile, their problems in conceiving children, and about their break-up. Fanica felt shivers down her spine. All this brought back the painful memory of the moment Vasile confessed he was in love with that bitch Elena Dresda. This was someone Fanica hated with passion. Her death hadn't done anything to diminish that feeling. But it didn't make her feel better either. Her heart had frozen when she lost Vasile, when her life became ordinary and uninteresting.

She didn't like the idea of talking about all that with the detectives from Bucharest. It was none of their business and she didn't want her past dug out simply for the sake of that that lunatic Amalia; a crazy woman, just like her mother. That family had been born to make decent people's lives miserable.

She was going to talk to Daria. Maybe she could convince the tall policeman with the ginger hair to stop interrogating her. At the end of the day, Vasile was dead and buried. What was the point of it all? Yes, that's what she would do.

Once she made up her mind, a sense of calmness descended upon her. Her mind opened to the universe around her. It was morning and it was chilly, but the clear sky hinted at a beautiful day to come. She gave the baker's son a cheerful greeting, and the boy answered with a grumpy remark, undoubtedly annoyed at having to go to work early. Fanica smiled at him. A baby's cry could be heard from an open window. Maybe Alexandra's daughter had given birth. That had to be it. Good grief, how time flies, Fanica thought and sighed. She stopped to buy a copy of *Libertatea* and a bar of rum-raisin chocolate. She carefully put them in her bag and continued on her way to work.

*

'I owe you a beer. A six-pack, even.'

Sergiu looked up from the computer's display and stared at his partner.

'Won the lottery or something?'

'My father-in-law answered my email. Well, he didn't reply to me directly, but he wrote to Mer. She called me this morning. She's overjoyed. That was good advice. Of course, there's a downside to it. Mer's mother is going to stay with us until the baby is born. But on the whole, it's positive.'

They hugged. Marius went out and bought coffees. Sergiu rolled a couple of cigarettes. He lit one, and passed the other to Marius.

'My wife is delighted,' Marius continued. 'She's already planning our first trip in three years to Istanbul. I miss that city, too. Have you ever been there?'

'Istanbul? No.'

'It's something else, let me tell you. It's full of life. Topkapi and Dolmabahce palaces are astonishing. As for the Basilica Cisterns… My cousin said Besiktasi are having a new stadium built, and they're digging a huge tunnel that will be a direct route to the Bosphorus. The little prick took photos. It really is spectacular. Meanwhile, in Bucharest they've been struggling for years to get a crappy road bridge done in Basarab.'

'I heard something about the stadium and the tunnel. Or maybe I read about it on the internet, can't remember.'

It annoyed Sergiu that he couldn't remember where he had picked up this information. In his line of work the source could sometimes be more important than the information.

*

Fanica sat very still. Only the constant nervous movement of her hands told them that she hadn't been frozen into a statue. It wasn't easy for her to talk about the man she had once loved; and probably still did. Yet it was also a relief, as if she had opened a door that had been sealed shut for too long, allowing the past to come bursting out into the open.

That thing about time healing all wounds is a fucking lie, Sergiu thought to himself as he watched and listened to the woman in front of him. Some wounds never heal.

Fanica's interrogation was a formal one. Dragos had already provided evidence that Amalia was not the forester's daughter. Although he had not been able to find the medical records for Fanica or Vasile, as medical archives that far back were in dusty paper files that had never been digitised, he had stumbled upon something else. The fertility specialist the couple had gone to all those years ago had published a study into infertility among young men, based on his many years of research. In the study, the subject was referred to as Vasile P, but there was no doubt about his real identity. Dragos had been highly amused as he had read how nervous and agitated the patient had been.

Sergiu left the interrogation to Marius. He turned to look out of the interview room's window. They had failed to fit all the pieces of the jigsaw together. This whole Amalia Dresda tale was getting on his nerves. If she wasn't the forester's daughter, who was her father? And what was her real role? It was becoming increasingly obvious that the clairvoyant business was a front, and a bad one at that. Where had she found the money for the apartment in Bucharest? The Voineasa house was sold after the purchase of the apartment and there was no evidence of any bank loan. They had found documentation relating to the purchase, but none concerning the sale of the house. How did the killings fit into the story? And were they her doing? All of them?

Sergiu left these questions unanswered and brought his wandering attention back to the room in the police headquarters.

'When you found out about Mr Petrache having a daughter, what was your reaction?' he heard Marius ask.

'That it was a prank,' Fanica replied. 'A ridiculous prank.'

*

Marius and Sergiu went out for a coffee. Fanica's 'ridiculous prank' comment stuck in their minds like an old song's refrain. The entire story looked like a prank to them.

'Two adults are being played by a youngster,' Marius growled.

'She's not just any kid. Obviously she's been trained.'

'By whom?'

'No idea.'

Sergiu was not being completely honest. He was starting sense a vaguely familiar scent. In the old folk tales, each vampire is able to sense another's presence. In the same way, he was picking up the scent of someone with the same training as his.

'It's a bit late…' he muttered to himself.

'What?'

'Nothing,' Sergiu answered, suspiciously quickly, looking up as the bartender approached.

'Excuse me, Mr. Manta? Mr Sergiu Manta?' he asked and they looked at him in surprise. 'You have a phone call, sir.'

'Where?'

'On the phone, of course.'

'I didn't presume it was on the coffee machine. Where's the phone, my friend?'

'My apologies, sir. It's on the right side of the bar.'

'Thank you.'

Sergiu got up and murmured to Marius as he passed.

'Don't look now, but we're being watched.'

Startled but not showing it, Marius turned around slowly. An old man nursing a glass of beer sat at the table to the right. The couple by the window seemed very much absorbed in one other. Next to them sat a pair of women, one young and the other middle-aged, neither of them looking particularly cheerful. Mother and daughter, Marius decided, probably with family business to look forward to.

'Which one of them?' Marius asked himself.

*

Sergiu grabbed the phone.

'Hello.'

'Sergiu? How are you?' a woman's voice asked, with fake cheer.

'I was drinking coffee and smoking. Who are you?'

'Smoking kills.'

'Coca Cola doesn't do any better. Again, who are you?'

'Manta, I'm really disappointed. You know the story of the old lady who was bored so she decided to teach her tomcat to speak? She tried everything. Private lessons, taking the animal to the theatre, having lunch together, sharing joints, you name it. All for nothing. The cat wouldn't speak. Until one day, the old lady and the cat were having coffee. The animal looked up and noticed that a piece of ceiling was broken and about to fall. So he called out to the woman to watch out. But she was so stunned that she didn't budge, and the ceiling caved in on her head, killing her on the spot. So the cat was disappointed, that after all those years of being taught to speak, when it finally did, she didn't listen.

'If the cat had been a man, he'd have expected it from the start... Amalia Dresda?'

'It took you a long time, partner.'

'Partner?'

'Don't tell me you bought that stuff about the astrology business?'

'No. And I didn't buy the love story with Modrogan either.'

Amalia didn't answer.

'How do I know you really are Amalia Dresda?' he asked.

'Because I'm the only one who ever shot at the great Sergiu Manta and is still alive to tell the tale,' she laughed.

'You're flattering me.'

'That wasn't my intention.'

'So what was your intention?'

'I wanted to know why you killed my mother? What were you expecting to achieve with that?'

Her voice had lost all its cheeriness.

'We didn't. Her death is the one that put us onto your trail. Why did you kill the others?'

'What others?'

'The others. Modrogan, Silviu, that poor old guy pretending to be your father.'

'Petrache wasn't my doing.'

'Then who did it?'

'You?'

'Why would we? After all, it was your parents' death which led us to you.'

'That's what you think. In fact, I'm on to you.'

'Amalia, we have to talk. The situation is serious and you're in deep shit.'

'And you're going to pull me out of it? I very much doubt it. I'm a contractor, just like you. I did as I was told. Now I'm no longer needed and my presence has become a liability. You were sent to take care of the problem."

'I wasn't…'

'Sergiu, drop it. It's not like I'm new to this.'

'Even if that's true, what can you do? You know I'm going to track you down sooner or later, right?'

'Yes, but I'm not going to make it easy for you. Or that policeman.'

'Suit yourself.'

'Sergiu?'

'Yes?'

'Is she any good?'

'Who?'

'Daria Modrogan.'

Sergiu hung up.

*

Sergiu took his seat at the table without a word. The look on his face was enough to tell Marius that something was wrong. He had plenty of questions to ask, but managed to swallow them down as Sergiu took out his phone and made a call.

'Hello, Dragos. We're in a place called Doris Café. I had a call on the land line there five minutes ago. Try to find the number the call was made from, please. No, how the hell should I know their landline number? C'mon, look things up, you're a big boy.'

He ended the conversation and threw the phone on the table.

'This girl is getting on my nerves,' Sergiu rasped.

'That was Amalia?'

'Yeah.'

'You're sure?'

'I've no reason to doubt her.'

'What did she say?'

Sergiu thought fast, deciding how much he could tell Marius, and aware that he would probably have to tell him everything, which would most likely end badly.

'She confirmed she was the one who took the pictures of Daria and me.'

'Why?'

'She didn't say. Most likely playing with us.'

'Did she say anything else?'

'She accused us of having killed her mother.'

'What? Is she insane? Why would we have done it?'

'No idea. But if she didn't do it, then someone else did. Someone with a grudge against Amalia. But who?'

'Daria?'

'That would mean she had done some research and discovered where the old lady lived in Bucharest, got over there and did her in. And for what? If she had murdered Amalia, it might have made some sense, but …'

'Sergiu, watch out. You are losing your objectivity about that woman.'

'Meaning?'

'You still consider her to be a victim in all this. But what if this isn't about hurt feelings, but something a lot more important? If we are to assume that relationships between these people are more than they appear to be, then we can't rule Mrs Modrogan out of this.'

Sergiu fell silent. What bothered him most was that the policeman was right. Daria was finding her way to his heart and that was not good. Not good at all.

CHAPTER SEVEN

'Ha!' Dragos squawked, jumping to his feet.

How on earth had he missed that? He had been focusing so much on the on the Voineasa finances that he had missed a crucial nugget of information that had been right there in front of him. But who'd have guessed? He reached for the mobile. Not the smartphone, the old-fashioned one with buttons.

'Hey, it's me, Dragos.'

'I know.'

'You know you asked me to dig into Mrs Modrogan's finances?'

'Yes.'

'Well, I did. There's nothing spectacular there. Her father made a lot of money during the Communist era, working for Dunarea. A lot of money for the time.

With the exception of the big house in Voineasa, the old man wasn't really much of a show-off. But what's weird is that when his daughter got married, he gave all the money to his son-in-law. She was left pretty much out in the cold, at least in legal terms.'

'That I know.'

'Hold on a minute. That thing with Stefan Gruia working at sea for his money? It doesn't add up. I'd bet that bar owner has no idea how to tie a bowline.'

'How so?'

'Well, this is supposed to have happened during the nineties. Formalities were out the window back then, it's true, but some old habits die hard. If he'd been part of a ship's crew, there would have been an official crew list. A couple of years back, employment records were computerised. Guess what? Mr Gruia is officially an employee of Internal Affairs.'

'Is? Like right now?'

'As we speak,' Dragos said. 'And it gets better. The money he presumably paid for Amalia's house came from Modrogan.'

'Maybe he wanted to discreetly help his girlfriend out.'

'Maybe. Except this happened long before the two of them got together, at least as far as I can make out. And we still don't know where Amalia got the money from to buy the apartment in Bucharest. No loans, from a bank or otherwise and no indication of where the money from the sale of the house in Voineasa went...'

'Oh, yes, we do know,' Sergiu said, and hung up.

*

'Get this into your thick skull. You're not to talk about this ever again. Not in the confessional, not when you're drunk, not even if your life depends on it. When this shit is done, you forget about me like we'd never met. That is if you care about yourself and the people you love.'

'Understood. But I still have to file a report about this case.'

'You'll get one already prepared.'

'This gang of yours doesn't muck around, does it?'

Sergiu didn't reply. His mind was still trying to cope with this new piece of information. It seemed that Amalia was part of his organisation. If he was to believe what she had said, someone else was responsible for her parents' deaths; very likely someone from the Agency. But who? And who had ordered it?'

The entire organisation that employed Sergiu was structured so that agents knew as little as possible about their colleagues and the rest of the Agency. In the course of carrying out the Agency's dirty work, he had got to know Dragos and a few other agents. The only manager he knew was Branescu, and up to that moment he had been comfortable with this arrangement, imagining that if he stayed clear of the others, they would do the same for him. he'd never considered the interests of those above him and possible conflicts between them. He realised that when the big guys failed to agree, they would never get their own hands dirty. They would send pawns, like him or Amalia, to fix things for them.

'Why would they want to kill her if she was one of yours?' Marius asked, scratching his head.

'I haven't a clue. Something went wrong. And now everyone's covering their tracks.'

'And Amalia's mother?'

'Don't know either. Maybe the girl played the rebel and they wanted to teach her a lesson. Or she knew too much. And when a good cop was sent in to investigate, all the alarm bells started to ring.'

Marius sighed.

'Somehow that compliment doesn't make me feel any better,' he said, while Sergiu brooded silently. 'Now I'm not surprised we couldn't get to her. She's good.'

'If her trainer was as good as mine, then she is really good.'

After recruitment, Sergiu had been through intensive training. The physical part had made him feel like he was back in the army, although he had to admit this time around it was a lot more reasonable and they were very keen to keep him healthy and fit. His IT knowledge was carefully checked, along with his technical skills and English. Then there had been lessons in German, French, Russian, communication technology, philosophy and psychology. For Sergiu this educational process had been a pleasure. His entire training was managed by Herr Bergen. He said he was German, but Sergiu suspected he was Romanian. The guy seemed to know everything. During the military training he had been tough and merciless, but apart from that he was the ideal teacher, capable of discussing literature, art, science, women and anything else.

With his training complete, Sergiu and Bergen spent a few months in Sölden in the Austrian mountains. Sergiu had played the part of a ski instructor, and Bergen was a rich tourist in need of coaching. It was a test of Sergiu's ability to blend in. That period of his life was one he looked back on fondly.

But if Amalia been given the same training, then she would be an opponent to be reckoned with.

*

Dragos took off his glasses and sighed. He had a special pair designed for the long hours in front of the screen, but he could still feel his eyes burning. After discovering details about Amalia Dresda's finances that he'd previously missed, he decided to run a second round of checks using the online sources he had available. That meant searching every database he could get into, legally or otherwise.

He took another sip of coffee. It seemed there was nothing new to find. And yet... An Amalia D was on the appointment list of an obstetrics gynaecology clinic. Dragos smiled, rubbed his hands, stretched his fingers and went back to the keyboard. There was fresh digging to be done.

*

The woman was running deep into the forest. The darkness and tree roots made her stumble. He could see her long black hair waving, but not her face. Every time she turned towards him, her hair was blown by the wind to cover her face. In spite of his efforts to catch her, she was always a few steps ahead of him. Sunlight made its way through the trees. As they were getting closer to the edge, a sunlight halo was beginning to appear around the girl's head that made her features even harder to distinguish. For one short moment she stopped and looked back at him. But he still couldn't see her where she was hidden against the light. He tried to reach her, but a sharp pain in his chest brought him to a standstill.

'Amalia! Wait!'

'Catch me!' she laughed and disappeared into the light.

Sergiu jolted awake, the dream still fresh in his mind. He could almost feel the pain that had taken his breath away while he was sleeping. He switched on the bedside light and checked his watch. 3:46. He got out of bed and walked to the bathroom where he splashed cold water on his face and arms. His mind started to work.

They say dreams are a subliminal response to everyday frustrations, problems and thoughts.

'Forest, Amalia, darkness…' Sergiu said out loud in an attempt to guess what the dream meant.

He turned off the water and reached for the towel to wipe his face. His eyes met his reflection in the mirror as he thought.

'You're an idiot!' he told his reflection, dropped the towel and hurried back to his room for his phone.

'Asleep?'

'Would it make any difference?'

'Not really. I need your magic digging skills.'

'I'm already digging. And got something.'

'Go on.'

'I stumbled upon an appointment Amalia Dresda made with an obstetrician. I looked into it and it seemed she went to the clinic on a regular basis. That suggests…'

'Pregnancy? Interesting. But here's what I need from you. Find out if Amalia, the bar owner, the forester, Daria or anyone else from this group owns a piece of forest.'

'On it.'

'Dragos?'

'Yeah?'

'Make it quick. If I'm right, Amalia is hiding in that forest. But she won't be there for long.'

Sergiu ended the conversation and sat on the bed. Since he couldn't sleep any longer, he put on a pair a shorts and a tee shirt and start exercising. Exertion always stimulated his mind.

'If I was Little Red Riding Hood and I stumbled upon the right wolf, I'd forget all about grandma and shack up in the forest with him,' he said to himself, repeating what she had told Gruia's son. 'They all thought it was just a joke. But what if it wasn't? Women like riddles and they like men to have a guess at them.'

*

'The long and the short of it is this,' Dragos began. 'A few years back, seven to be precise, Vasile Petrache handed in a planning application to build a cabin in the woods. The chosen spot was named The Priest's Nest by the locals. There was a legend about a priest who'd lived in these parts before World War Two. He was very involved with the community and people really loved him. But he had bad luck. His wife got tuberculosis in 1938 and died. From that moment on the man went nuts. He abandoned his work, built a place in the forest and lived off-grid long before it became fashionable. People who kept in touch with him said he talked about phantoms and all kinds of horror stories. He never left the place and died in 1942. Back to the present day, and our forester wanted to build a small house and organise special weekends in the haunted woods for the horror-loving tourists.'

'Interesting idea. Where did he get the money for it?'

'Well, that's the interesting part. He didn't. Petrache was going to manage the place. The project was to be financed by the Blue Poplar Company, the one that legally owned...'

'The bar of the same name. Why would Gruia finance Petrache's business? As far as we know, the forester wasn't exactly trustworthy.'

'I suppose this is why it never got past the project phase.'

'Do you think you can pinpoint the place for me?'

'The documentation included a map. Based on that I could determine an approximate location. I'll send you the co-ordinates.'

'Thanks, Dragos. Sorry to interrupt your beauty sleep.'

'No worries. When we're done with this I'll take a week of and sleep all the way through it.'

Sergiu laughed out loud, hung up and left in a hurry. By now it was just after six and with luck he could put an end to the whole matter before everyone else had finished their first cup of morning coffee.

*

Marius opened the door of the office they occupied in the local police headquarters. Relu Dobre was already in there, staring out through the window, drinking a coffee and smoking a cigarette made out of Sergiu's tobacco.

'Hello? Sergiu isn't here?'

'I thought he was with you.'

'Haven't seen him since last night. He didn't show up at breakfast either. Where the hell is he?'

'Maybe he's with Mrs Modrogan,' Relu grinned.

'Maybe,' Marius answered, unconvinced. 'Any news?'

'I beg your pardon?'

'I presume you were waiting for us.'

'Well, yes. I did what Sergiu told me to. I checked Petrache's past. Not that it was that there was much to check. But I found something that could be interesting. A few years back he tried to set up a business with a cabin in the woods. It was all based on a tale about a priest who lived around here before the war. But the story is that the guy went crazy out there in the woods, living like a monk. Petrache had hoped to make some money out of it. Not a hope, if you ask me. But, what's interesting is that a couple of months back Gruia applied to have permission for the project renewed.'

'Gruia? The Blue Poplar's owner? Why?'

'He was Petrache's business partner.'

'Really? I'd never guessed a partnership like that was even a possibility.'

'Yeah, it looks odd.'

'Thanks for the info.'

'You're welcome.'

Marius said no more, hoping Relu would be on his way and he could have a chance to put his thoughts in order. Relu sensed what Marius was thinking and slipped out of the room. Marius opened the window and lit a cigarette. What was with this cabin in the woods story? How had Voineasa's very own Kenny

Rogers become that loser Petrache's business partner? And where the hell was Sergiu?

*

The girl walked fast, with quick, light steps, constantly looking around her. She couldn't escape the feeling someone was there, in the woods, on her tail. She had woken up with a feeling of uneasiness that hadn't left her all morning. Even the time spent with her baby was not enough to restore her peace of mind. After that she met Rares to pick up the groceries from him and saw that the boy was genuinely scared. The investigation, the detective from Bucharest who wouldn't leave him alone, and the everlasting quarrels with Gruia had all combined to make him very tense indeed.

She knew she had to calm him down. The solution was sex, right there on the spot, under the sky, behind the Blue Poplar itself. She hadn't really been in the mood and he was far too agitated, so the result was something brief and unsatisfactory, at least for her. But Rares was much calmer afterwards, and that was important. She needed him.

After that she took the bag of groceries from him and left for the hideaway in the woods. On the way she stopped at a small store and bought a bottle of Jim Beam. She was anxious too. Once she reached the forest, she noticed fresh footprints. These could have been left by one of the foresters, but her gut told her otherwise. Now she could see the house among the trees. She reached for the gun hidden in her belt, under her coat. It was a small, girlish pistol, but it gave her a feeling of security. She had always had a liking for firearms. When she was a child, Petrache took her hunting with him; well, not exactly hunting. Once the winter passed they would walk through the forest and kill the sick animals. She didn't mind doing that and knew it was a good thing to do. They were spared the suffering of a long and painful death, and she loved feeling the weapon in her hand, pulling the trigger and feeling the gun kick back.

She stepped on the small porch and a board creaked under her foot, the one she had been meaning to fix for weeks. She was starting to behave more and more like a man. She opened the door and went to put the bags on the table. She was two steps from it when the sound of a voice stopped her.

'Amalia. I'm glad we finally meet face to face.'

*

Two short knocks and the door of the office Relu Dobre shared with other two colleagues opened wide. Topped by his unruly mop of hair, Marius's head appeared in the doorway.

'Relu, I'm sorry to bother you, but could we have a word?'

'Sure.'

Relu followed Marius out into the corridor.

'I was wondering if you could approach the mayor's office for me. I'd like to see the file on Petrache's business with that cabin in the woods. I want to question Gruia about it, but I need solid information rather than merely hearsay to back it up.'

'Already done it. I'll bring you the copy I have. I meant to do it this morning, but you seemed worried by your partner's absence. Did he show up?'

'No. And I'm worried. He's not answering his phone. And all those missed calls from me should tell him it's important.'

'It's a hell of a partnership you two have...'

'We're not really partners. We work at different stations. They had us working together for this case only.'

'I see,' Dobre said He was tempted to ask what case, but he thought better of it.

'Wait here. I'll bring you the file.'

Waiting for Relu, Marius let his mind work. Sergiu must have already heard about the cabin in the woods, most likely from that computer wizard of theirs, and had gone chasing Amalia by himself; no doubt so they could settle things privately. A part of his brain was screaming at him to stay out of it and leave them to their little spy games. He was aware he already knew too much for his own good. But he had no choice. He couldn't allow the super-agent to eliminate the only suspect in a multiple homicide case. He simply couldn't.

*

Amalia sat demurely, hands in her lap. Still as she was, eyes on the man in front of her, she could almost pass as a lovestruck teenager – almost. On the table beside her lay the small gun with the silver handle and the commando knife. The bullets were all lined up on the floor. Sergiu had finally got to the bottom of the story.

Amalia shared it calmly, without a trace of sentimentality. Her birth was the result of a drinking spree and a fumbled fuck between Gruia and Elena Dresda. The only problem was that the man was still deeply in love with Daria, so Amalia's mother hadn't wasted any time on him. Once she realised she was pregnant, she accepted Petrache, who had not hesitated to leave Fanica. For a while they played happy families, but after a period, things went downhill. Elena's indiscretions hadn't helped. In the meantime, Gruia had been dumped by Daria in favour of a man with better prospects. So he found a girl, shy and poor, married her and became a father sooner than expected.

'But the kid was not his.'

'He wasn't. You knew?'

'Yes. Gruia told us. Well, he told my partner.'

'Your partner. I see…'

'How did you find out about it?' Sergiu asked, unwilling to talk about the detective he was working with.

"My mother told me, and that gave me an idea. I knew the man was up to something. There was no way a loser like him could get his hands on that kind of money by himself. I told him I wanted in, or I was going to spread the word I was his daughter. And I'd also tell Rares he fucked his sister. I think was what swung it. Gruia really loves Rares, even if he's not his real father.'

'That's how you got to work for the Agency?'

Amalia nodded.

'At first there were trivial assignments, just courier work, meeting contacts, things like that. Then Petrache turned into a loose cannon. He drank a lot, smoked a lot and then came home and beat the hell out of my mother. One time he banged her head against the table and almost killed her. That's when I told Gruia I wanted to take her out of town. He got money from the Agency to buy my mother's house so that I could buy the apartment in Bucharest. Their condition was that I became a full agent. I had no objection. It wasn't as if I had any better options.'

'Did Branescu manage you?'

Amalia smiled.

'No. Branescu is only one of the pawns. He thinks of himself as a big boss, but he's in for a surprise pretty soon. You can't ditch the top brass that easily.'

So it's the age-old rivalry and jostling between groups for influence, Sergiu thought. He personally didn't give a damn about who was who within the Agency. When Branescu got him out of prison to make him an operative for their dirty work, he had thought Branescu was the man in charge. Over time he realised there had to be more of a hierarchy, but he didn't waste much time thinking about it. He had to work with Branescu and a few other people. Apart from that he kept to himself and hoped the others would do the same. But this status quo couldn't last. The upper levels were moving their pieces in the board, and Sergiu and the rest of the agents were the pawns. Or the bishops...

'The Modrogan affair was a mission?'

'At the beginning, yes. The Agency needed someone with influence in government and money to ensure some sort of backup. They sent me to seduce and recruit him. At first he was flattered. He'd been suffering from heavy depression back then. He was in the middle of a divorce and engaged to a woman who proved to be shallow and materialistic. But the politics weren't quite what he had expected. We know this is not a game. Modrogan soon discovered it too. He started going off the rails. The Agency's orders were to calm him down at all costs. Or kill him. There was one problem.'

'You were in love with him?'

'Was it that obvious?'

'The scene you made when you found out about Modrogan's engagement was. I know it was meant to show everyone you had gone, yet all the people who witnessed it were sort of impressed. Relu blocked any investigation into you, Daria got scared enough to involve the police. The reason she didn't press charges was because Gruia talked her out of it. Well, him being your real father explains it.'

Amalia sighed.

'I admit, it caught me off guard. I really thought he loved me and that I had managed to get that blonde bitch out of the picture. How wrong can you be? People like us should never fall in love.'

'That's true. Was this when you decided to kill him?'

'Yes ... No ... I don't know. I guess I always knew we weren't for real, but I just didn't want to admit it.

Stefan was pissing off the people in the Agency and they were all over me with it. On top of it, I noticed he was being tailed.'

'Silviu? That's why you hit on him?'

'It wasn't that hard. I found out what gym he was attending and joined. From that moment on it was a piece of cake. He wasn't our finest,' she smiled.

'But he was one of us. And you eliminated him.'

'Without an order, you mean. Unlike you. They actually sent you here for this job.'

Sergiu tried to reply, but she stopped him with a gesture. She stood up, stepped closer and looked him in the eyes.

'What the hell do you think is going on? The big guys are playing for some kind of showdown, that's what's going on. Ileana Munteanu, my trainer, has been after Branescu's position for years. She formed her own team within the Agency. And she's got all the people Branescu dismissed behind her, like Gruia or even your beloved Daria.'

'Why are you telling me this? Why don't you just try to kill me?'

Amalia returned to her seat with an exhausted look on her face.

'What would be the point? Assuming I'd manage to

kill you, they'd send someone else to finish the job. The stars are in favour of your boss these days. But I wouldn't count on that if I were you. The signs have a weird sense of humour. Take it from someone who knows this shit. But I have a request. My baby girl. You must help her, find her family.'

'Me?'

'Who else? She's Modrogan's child, but I doubt Daria would want to have her. The Perjas look after her, but they won't be doing that when the money stops. She'll end up in an orphanage. And you know what that's like.'

Amalia was about to say more, but the sound of the creaking board outside stopped her. Someone was at the door.

CHAPTER EIGHT

They fell silent and waited. A second later Marius appeared in the doorway. Before he could even blink, Amalia snatched the commando knife and slashed at the policeman's throat. Instinctively, Sergiu fired twice. Amalia sank back dead in the chair, eyes wide open, one bullet in her head, the other in her chest. Marius tried to speak, but only a helpless gurgle came from his throat before he collapsed, his eyes wide open.

Could he have done anything differently, Sergiu asked himself afterwards. Could he have stopped Amalia from killing Marius? When the girl had come into the cabin, he'd been waiting for her. He had her covered, so she had to put her knife and gun down. Why had he then left them on the table? Why hadn't he moved them out of her reach? Was it because he knew he was there to take her down and he would have felt like a bastard if he hadn't given her some slight chance to defend herself? Was it because he had hoped that Marius would show up? He didn't want to admit it to himself, but as far as the Agency would be concerned, this was ending convenient tied up the loose ends. Marius had known too much about the Agency. He would have had to have been eliminated one way or the other, simply for doing his job well.

*

'Care to share?' Dragos asked, pointing at the bottle.

Sergiu passed it to him. Dragos took a slug and grimaced.

'Can't believe this mess is so close to home.'

'Power corrupts. Branescu has a powerful position. Sooner or later, someone is going to want to step into his shoes. It was our mistake to think that if we mind our own business, this skirmish wouldn't affect us. We're the foot soldiers. If they're waging a war…'

'…we're the ones doing the fighting,' Dragos said and fell silent. 'So all these killings were, in fact, jobs?' he said at last.

'Modrogan was her target to begin with. But he died because he'd betrayed her.'

'Shit. I should be more careful with women.'

'Yes, you should.'

'What about Silviu?'

'Silviu had the misfortune to play for the other team. And he was faced with quite an opponent. Better than he was, anyway.'

'And her parents?'

'Petrache was an arsehole. He knew Amalia wasn't his daughter. He was furious when she and her mother moved to Bucharest. He must have figured out that once the house was sold, Amalia would be using the cabin in the woods when she was here. He chanced upon her there and that was his last mistake. As for the mother, I think she was eliminated by our people.'

'But why?'

Sergiu shrugged.

'To scare Amalia, I presume. The funny thing is she had no idea about it until I told her.'

'And the marks on the bodies?'

'She punched Modrogan with her fist. The ring made the impression. When she killed Silviu she thought she could connect the hits and create a false trail to confuse any investigation.'

'And our people used that to pin her mother's death on her as well? I wonder which colleague of ours did her in.'

'Does it matter? It was ordered, anyway.'

'Yeah, it stinks. Branescu told me he expects a report on Relu. Whether he's any use to us or not.'

'Only if he learns to keep his mouth shut. He talks more than any woman I've ever known.'

'Should I dig some info on Amalia's boss, this Ileana Munteanu? To help Branescu watch his back.'

'We tell him what we know about Amalia. Other than that, let him watch his own back. We'll be pretty busy watching ours,' Sergiu said and stood up.

'Where are you going?'

'I have one last thing to do before we leave.'

'You're too drunk to drive.'

'Then get in the car and drive me.'

Dragos didn't wait to be told twice. He knew Sergiu didn't make a habit of repeating himself.

*

'Why on earth would I do that?' Rares asked looking at Sergiu as if he'd just landed from another planet.

'Because there's no one else. And this is the most important thing you can do for Amalia.'

'Everything is about Amalia, isn't it? Well, it was, I suppose. Help her get the luggage in the car, bring her the camera in the middle of the night. Can you picture me raising a kid?'

'If Amalia had showed up pregnant at your door, would you have been better prepared to become a parent? Do you think watching her belly swell would have given you some insight into parenthood?'

'This baby girl? Is she mine?'

'You'll bring her up, be by her side when she cries, you'll drive her to school and get your first gun when a pimpled little prick like you shows up on your doorstep to take her out. Whose kid could she be? Rares, have you ever visited an orphanage? Well, I grew up in one. I could spend days telling you about humiliation and violence. No, not the staff. The other kids. Everything was a reason for a fight; a toy, a sweet, a quiet place. As for the staff, they were unappreciated, underpaid, had no resources and they were sick of everything. That child is all Amalia left behind.'

Rares didn't answer. He kept polishing the motorbike as if he was trying to strip the paint off it. Sergiu got up and started walking slowly to the door.

'You know, there was a time I really thought this could have worked out,' the boy said, and Sergiu halted in the doorway. 'Amalia and her mother had already moved to Bucharest. She came to town and wanted to stay at my place. I was living at the old man's house back then, and he wouldn't have it. That's when I decided to move out here, in the garage. Amalia went to the cabin and found Petrache there. He was drunk and they had a fight. Amalia told him she knew he wasn't her father. That's when he attacked her. My girl was not the damsel-in-distress type. She beat the shit out of him. But she was worried, because she couldn't stay at my place and she had no money for a hotel. So she had to use the cabin. She was afraid Petrache could take her by surprise somehow. I didn't want her to be afraid. I was already feeling like a wimp because I couldn't stand up for her in front of my father. So I followed Petrache when he left the bar and cornered him in an alley. I was only going to knock him about a bit, frighten him. I didn't know the idiot had a knife. How could I? He cut my arm. But I was younger, stronger and sober. I managed to get the knife off him and pushed him away. He hit his head against the pavement and that was it. When I called Amalia she couldn't believe it. She didn't think I had it in me. Frankly, neither did I. It was her idea to dump him in the ravine by the forest. I thought this would bring us together. But attraction for Modrogan was too strong,' Rares said and sighed.

Sergiu walked around the bike, his finger pressed against his lips. He stopped behind Rares and put a hand on his shoulder.

'I've no idea what you are talking about. Amalia told me she killed Petrache in self-defence.'

Rares stopped polishing and stared at him in astonishment.

'She did?'

'Yes, she did,' Sergiu said, his hand on the young man's shoulder.

'Then that must be the truth.'

Rares wiped his face with his sleeve.

Sergiu was still behind him, but he could swear he saw tears on the sleeve. Sergiu took a note from his pocket and put it on the Ij.

'The Perjas' address and phone number. Call them and go get your daughter. And when she grows up, give her these and tell her they belonged to her mother.'

Rares watched Sergiu place a zodiac engraved pendant and ring by the note. The boy closed the door behind Sergiu. He went over to the bike, took the ring and kissed it. Only then did he burst into tears.

*

'Yes, I admit. You're a real estate mastermind. And a diplomat as well, since you convinced Branescu to pay the rent for that place.'

'Well I think he felt a bit guilty about this joint investigation with the police and the way it ended up. Not the smartest idea he ever had.'

'Yeah, about that, I was thinking…'

The sound of the landline phone ringing cut their conversation short. Dragos went in to answer. Sergiu stayed on the terrace and rolled himself a cigarette.

'Yes, that's me. What? Shit, when was that? Are you absolutely sure? Hell! I'll tell him.'

Dragos put down the phone and got back on the terrace. Sergiu was blowing smoke rings. Dragos stopped and scratched his head, wondering what the right words might be.

'Out with it,' Sergiu growled. 'I can see from your face that it's bad news.'

'Laura intercepted a conversation on police radio frequency. A murder at the Finnish Club, you know, city centre. The victim's name is Alina Stanescu.'

'Fuck!'

Sergiu's face turned pale and his breath came in gasps.

'It seems that arsehole of a boyfriend came for her at the club. He had a gun and shot her on the spot. Jealousy.'

'Yeah, right,' Sergiu snarled.

'Sergiu, it wasn't us. It just happened. I didn't say a word about you and her. You have to believe me.'

'I'll believe you kept your mouth shut. But I don't believe in coincidences. Her boyfriend having a fit of jealousy just as the Agency is tying up loose ends? I'm not buying that.'

'They have proof it was her boyfriend.'

'Dragos, please. How hard can be to convince a guy like that that his girl is cheating on him? An anonymous message, a photo, anything goes.'

'I don't know what to say.'

'Then don't say anything.'

Sergiu shrugged on his jacket.

'Where are you going?'

'To get some air.'

'You have to take care of a problem for me first,' a voice said from the doorway.

They turned to see Branescu standing there. Dragos wondered how long he'd been standing there and how much of the conversation he had heard. It was no wonder Sergiu was so paranoid about him.

'Stop sneaking around like that,' Sergiu snapped at him. 'You'll get a bullet in the head one day.'

'That day isn't here yet,' Branescu replied.

*

It was like a scene from a film as they faced each other. Daria kept her hands on the table and looked down at them.

'You wanted to see me. Why?' Sergiu asked.

She raised her eyes and smiled sadly.

'I missed you.'

Sergiu didn't answer, but she could see the awkwardness on his face. He was no fan of declarations of love, and it seemed to him that Daria's were a little over the top. He was convinced she'd led him on, hoping to influence his judgement.

'Don't get sentimental with me, Daria. It won't work.'

'Why? Agency men don't have feelings?'

'Don't they?'

'You mean our time together was all part of a game?'

Sergiu scowled.

'Daria, you were attracted by a detective determined to get to the bottom of your husband's death. I was attracted by a lonely and vulnerable widow. Neither of us was what we seemed to be.'

'Does it always have to be black and white with you? Well, here's news for you, life is about shades of grey. True, I made a move on you because I needed protection. But what we had was real for me. Wasn't it for you?'

Sergiu didn't answer straight away.

'What we had couldn't last,' he said finally. 'You know that.'

'I know,' she said, with a dismissive gesture. 'That's why I wanted to see you. It seems they're taking me away for debriefing. I have no idea when I'll be able to see you again.'

All Sergiu wanted was for the meeting to be over. But he also wished to leave her with a happy memory, knowing that she was in for some complicated times. In this business when you change sides, it can be difficult and stressful while the new employer extracts information. He had been the interrogator often enough to be aware of this. He also knew that the two rivals co-existing within the same unit would make things even harder for Daria. He took her hand and kissed it gently, held it for a while, then looked into her eyes.

'Take care.'

Daria smiled. Sergiu got up to leave the room, but her frightened voice stopped him in his tracks.

'I'm scared. What's going to happen to me?'

'Play it straight and you'll be fine,' Sergiu told her, trying to sound convincing.

'They took Gruia as well. I won't be seeing him either, you know.'

Sergiu didn't answer. He knew from experience that the loneliness would get to Daria.

'Thank you,' Branescu said as Sergiu closed the door behind him. 'I know this wasn't easy for you.'

'It wasn't. What's going to happen to her?'

'She has potential. We'll debrief her, and then we train her. She'll be fine.'

Sergiu thought that if her training were to be anything like his, she would be very unhappy. But he said nothing.

*

Anyone might be forgiven for mistaking Dragos for a student wracked with nervous anxiety before an exam. He paced the hall outside Branescu's office, a file in his hands, muttering to himself. He had spent the last few days digging for information. The Amalia affair had identified a rival faction within the Agency, and its leader, Ileana Munteanu. He had dug as deep as he dared and as discreetly as he could to find out who she really was, and which of the Agency's people were backing her.

Up to that moment, both he and Sergiu had kept away from internal politics, reasoning that what you don't know can't hurt you. They had both been wrong. The moment the factions had decided to settle scores, it was not the leaders who would bear the consequences, but the agents assigned to murder each other. Dragos had racked his brains over whether to provide his boss with the full information about his adversary.

Dragos was just debating whether to go through with it or not, when the office door got opened and Branescu appeared.

'Mr Apostolescu. Are you looking for me?'

'Yes, well, I…'

Dragos didn't get to finish his sentence. A woman appeared from behind his boss.

'I'm glad we had this conversation, Mr Branescu,' she said smoothly. 'It was necessary, I hope there won't be any communication breakdowns in the future. It's too expensive for all of us.'

'I agree entirely.'

Dragos forced himself not to stare as he recognised Ileana Munteanu saying goodbye to Branescu.

'You wished to talk to me?'

'Yes, sir,' Dragos said, marshalling his thoughts. 'I was wondering if it is all right to set up some rest and recuperation for Sergiu. I have some options, but I wanted your approval before showing them to him.'

'A vacation? After getting that fancy apartment for him?'

'Well I thought that…'

'Fine! As long as it's nothing expensive. And make sure it's close by, in case I need him.'

'Thank you, sir. I'll talk to him and let you know.'

Branescu nodded approval, and disappeared back into his office, firmly shutting the door behind him.

Dragos took deep breaths while he tried to think through what he had just seen.

'Surprises like that will be the death of me,' he muttered to himself.

*

'Not a driver, are you? You're just like your father. When you grow up, you'll be a rider.'

The girl put her hands on the young man's face and smiled to show him her two front teeth. When he lifted her into his arms she stopped crying and her laughter brought a lump to his throat.

'You have a beautiful little girl.'

He turned suddenly. The little girl's eyes followed as they both wondered who the gentleman in the black suit might be. The father's eyes took in the black car behind the man, a shiny new Volvo.

'The car looks all right…'

'It is. It's not the car that brought me here, it was you,

Rares Gruia. In fact, allow me to drive you home. I think you live in your father's house now, which is far more comfortable for the little girl. Once we get there, in exchange for a coffee and a glass of water, I'll make you an offer that gives you the chance of a decent future for you and your child. For someone with your potential, it shouldn't be a problem.'

Rares blinked a few times. The little girl registered that her father's attention was elsewhere.

'I seem to be at disadvantage here,' Rares said after a while. 'You seem to know me. Or about me, at least. I don't even know your name.'

'Of course, my apologies. My name is Branescu and I work for the Ministry of Internal Affairs,' the man in the suit said.

*

Sergiu was strolled past shop windows on a cool but pleasant evening, without taking in much of what was on display. Since he moved he'd made a habit of taking an occasional walk through the city centre. He enjoyed people watching in the streets, the bars, the clubs, the shops. He listened to people talking and made up stories based on these fragments of other people's lives. Maybe it had something to do with his age, he wondered, or with him not having a life of his own and instead stealing pieces of other people's existences. Sergiu's thoughts were prone to wander. But he decided he was fine. Today would be a good day. He had slept until noon and then taken his bike through the city, even taking the chance to cruise past the building where his wife and son lived. He had been lucky and had seen them just coming out of the main door, looking cheerful and content.

Afterwards he went to the book launch, not something he would usually do. He wasn't one for events like these, and neither was he much interested in crime stories, preferring science fiction or fantasy. But this was a book he had heard about, written by a young woman. Although the author was only in her early twenties, she had already written four books. What had intrigued Sergiu was that although these books were written as fiction, each one was based on a true fact, using a well-known crime as a starting point. She had earned a little notoriety as it was assumed she had a source somewhere in official circles which enabled her to get the details right.

This latest novel of hers had caught Sergiu's eye because it was based on the intriguing case of four Romanian guys who had paid a visit to the Kunsthal museum in Rotterdam a few years before. Then one October night they came back, walked in as if they owned the place and helped themselves to seven paintings worth eighteen million euros. Nobody ever figured out how those burglars had managed to pull this off. Later on, there were rumours that it had been an insurance scam and that they had inside help. Sergiu was curious which theory Irina Grosu would espouse.

He'd had enough of walking, so he decided to take the metro. At the Universitate station, when he saw how crowded it was, he nearly changed his mind, but now it was too late. Once he got on the train, he chose a corner that seemed a little less crowded. Near the door there was a girl who was also trying to read. Every now and then someone would bump into her and she would lose her place on the page. Every time this happened she would frown without looking up. Finally, a man built like a sumo wrestler jostled her on his way past and the book fell to the floor. Sergiu scowled at the man, picked up her book and smiled to himself as he saw the title. *The Colours of Ash* by Irina Grosu.

The girl was pretty, a tinge of purple to her dark hair, and large round glasses on a snub nose surrounded by freckles. When she smiled, her face lit up. As the next station approached, she stowed the book away in her backpack and shrugged on her coat. Sergiu lifted the woman's bag and handed it to her.

'What are you carrying? Rocks?'

'No, books,' she laughed. 'I was at the library and picked up the books I need for a paper.'

'You don't believe in e-readers?'

'Sure. But I'm old school. I prefer paper.'

'Tree killer!'

The train juddered to a halt the station, and the girl lost her balance, ending up in Sergiu's arms. She mumbled an apology, smiled again and left as quickly as she could. On instinct, Sergiu checked his pocket.

I'm Diana. Maybe we could meet and talk about the book, had been hastily written on a bookmark, along with a mobile number, and Sergiu laughed to himself.

*

Sergiu didn't spend much time watching television. Back when he had been living in Brasov, he hadn't even had one. But since moving to the new place, he had slipped into got the habit of watching documentaries now and then, and sometimes news digests on the big plasma screen that had come with the flat. Apart from that, the place was sparsely furnished with a leather armchair that was a lot less comfortable then it looked, a small wooden table for a desk and a chair to go with it. Sergiu had brought the hi-fi and the books, still stored in four Ikea boxes, as the apartment didn't have any bookshelves. He toyed with the thought of moving the bed into the living room, but he gave up on the idea. To start with, the bed weighed a ton and in any case, he had no desire to sleep in the same room where he liked to smoke.

Sergiu dropped his boots in the hall, draped his biker's jacket over the chair in the living room and switched on the television. He was about to collapse into the armchair, but he changed his mind. Went to the kitchen and came back with a glass and a half full bottle of Jim Beam, stumbling over his own boots, and cursed as he kicked them down the hallway. He tapped the crystal glass with his fingernail before pouring himself a drink. When it came to home comforts, there wasn't much to be found in this apartment, but a kitchen cupboard revealed a set of six Bohemia crystal glasses. It tickled Sergiu's sense of humour to be eating off disposable plates while drinking from fancy glasses. After the first sip of whisky he let himself fall back into the armchair.

One channel was showing *Independence Day*, another one had a soap opera and third was showing a Turkish movie. A Romanian channel had an interminable discussion over something the Prime Minister was supposed to have said, and he scrolled on to the EuroNews with its report of a car bomb that had been detonated in Istanbul. There had been three fatalities, and the report that one of them had been a heavily pregnant woman caught Sergiu's attention. The explosion had occurred in a tunnel, with a great deal of damage and numerous injuries.

There was something about the report that stuck in Sergiu's thoughts. He had a gut feeling that this was important and he scanned other news channels for more information. There was nothing on CNN, and an hour later, one of Romania's most popular channels, PRO TV, had included the same information in its news bulletin. He switched to searching the internet, and the pieces came together in his mind. He recalled Marius mentioning that his cousin had photographed the new tunnel in Istanbul, the city for which the Agency's training officer had such a liking. Bergen had often mentioned his affection for Istanbul during their nights in Sölden when they had played chess and swapped stories.

*

The aircraft landed at 16.40. He stood for a long time in line at the passport control point. Usually, Romanian customs were fairly quick, but this time the customs officers had taken their time shaking down a couple of passengers with Arabic names and looks, which had held everyone up. It hadn't helped that three flights had landed within a few minutes of each other at Bucharest's Henri Coanda airport and only one of the baggage carousels was working. After twenty minutes of being pushed and shoved as if the arrivals hall was a supermarket on the first day of the sales, he finally retrieved his brown leather suitcase.

It was just after 17.30 when the grey bearded gentleman with a raincoat and hat discovered the taxi ordering machines and saw this as a long overdue improvement. The last time he had been in Bucharest a crook of a cab driver had charged him a fortune for the trip from the airport to Victoria Plaza. But arriving at two in the morning had left him with little choice.

The man followed the instructions and called a taxi. The machine displayed the car number, the charge, name, picture and rating of the driver, and a few minutes later he was collected by middle-aged taxi driver Valeriu Popescu. Ten minutes later they were close to centre of Otopeni, the suburb of Bucharest of which the airport is the main feature. This was where things slowed down, the roads were heavily clogged with traffic. He reflected that Romanians had to really enjoy spending time in their cars. At the traffic light at the end of the bridge, the passenger looked at the No Smoking sign and sighed.

'Don't take any notice of that,' the driver said. 'The taxi company made us put the signs up. It's fine to smoke as long as you open the window.'

'Thanks,' his passenger said with relief, plucking a packet of Gitanes from his pocket and offering one to the driver.

'I wouldn't say no.'

They smoked in silence for a while.

'You come home often?'

'Is it that obvious I'm Romanian?'

'You speak Romanian very well. I used to teach Romanian language and literature at the Caragiale college, before I had to switch to driving a taxi instead to make ends meet. Anyway, I notice these things. You speak correctly, but also with ease, so that tells me you're a native speaker,' Valeriu Popescu explained while his passenger nodded, not keen to be drawn into a discussion.

By the time they reached the modern building that served as temporary headquarters for the city's First District administration, the traffic light brought them to another halt. The bearded gentleman took off his hat and gazed out of the window. He had noticed the presence of a red and black motorcycle, one of those lightweight Japanese ones, among the cars and buses making slow progress against the traffic. Its rider was all in black, even the man's visor was smoked glass and a bandana with a skull motif covered the lower half of the man's face. All the same, there was something familiar about this figure.

Just before the lights turned green, the rider lifted his visor and pulled the bandana down as he looked sideways. He had a small wooden tube the size of a pencil in one hand.

'Good night, Mr Bergen,' the rider said, putting the tube to his lips and blowing swiftly.

Half of an hour later, Valeriu Popescu almost had a heart attack when he discovered that the passenger in the back seat was now a corpse.

*

There had been no doubt in his mind, from the moment he remembered who had told him about that tunnel in Istanbul. He knew that the pregnant car bomb victim had to be Marius's wife and he assumed that the other two were her parents. After the policeman's death, Sergiu hadn't tried to check up on Meryem. He found it impossible to even think about her, weighed down with guilt as he was. But it made sense that after losing her husband she would have sought refuge at her parents' home, especially since they had recently put aside their differences.

After finding out everything he could about the explosion from television news reports and the internet, Sergiu had gone to Dragos to find out where his former trainer was living.

A call at five in the morning had confirmed what he had suspected in one word. Istanbul. Sergiu needed no further proof. Two days later, Dragos let him know that Bergen was due to arrive in Bucharest, and the flight number gave him the date and time.

Now facing Branescu, Sergiu was being given the sad news of his former trainer's unexpected death, knowing that his boss would be searching for any kind of reaction.

'Do we know who did it?' Sergiu asked, putting on his best poker face.

Branescu raised an eyebrow.

'No. We don't.'

Sergiu didn't say anything else. He was about to leave the room when Branescu stopped him.

'Sergiu.'

'Yes?'

'You're all right, aren't you?'

'Yeah.'

*

Sergiu was tired. So much so that he crashed into the armchair in the living room and fell asleep, still wearing his leathers and boots. It was three in the morning when he woke, cold and numb. He switched off the television, went to the kitchen and poured the last drop of whisky into a glass. Opening the balcony door, he enjoyed listening to the wind blowing the leaves off the trees in the inner yard of the building. He was still cold, so he fetched his jacket, zipped it up and started rolling himself a cigarette. He fumbled in his pocket for a lighter.

'Shit,' Sergiu growled as he felt for the lighter that had slipped through a hole in the lining of his jacket. Instead, he found something else, the bookmark the girl on the subway had slipped into his pocket. He remembered her; petite, funny coloured hair, snub nose, big blue eyes. Or were they green? A sweet thing, anyway. Sergiu looked at the phone number she had written and smiled, for a second. Then Alina came to mind. He frowned, held the bookmark over his lighter and dropped it in the ashtray where he watched it burn.

He lit his cigarette and took a sip of whisky, played with the smoke and watched the world outside. The entire yard was living in the dark, all except the apartment opposite on the second floor. An old man lived there and Sergiu liked to watch him taking care of his plants now and then. But three in the morning was a peculiar time for horticulture, he decided, and then there was that strange light in that balcony. He went inside and picked up his binoculars, focusing on the neighbour's balcony. He smiled as he saw that the old man was looking after his own homegrown recreational substances. Wasn't that sweet?

'Dragos really knows how to pick places for me,' Sergiu grunted to himself.

ACKNOWLEDGEMENTS

Writing a book is a solitary occupation. There are few things in life more personal than writing. Nevertheless, no book ever appears in this world without a collective effort. No matter how talented he or she may be, an author has to acknowledge that the people around him or her make an important contribution.

This book is no exception to the rule, so I would like to thank those who, consciously or not, helped Sergiu Manta to come into existence.

First of all, thank you, Orlando. Your personality, attitude and the stories you shared in front of a glass of wine (me) and a beer (you) inspired me in creating Sergiu Manta. I'm not sure how you feel about it, but I'm very happy.

My cousin, Radu, the man I share books with and then comment on them late into the night, as I did with my father long ago. He was the very first reader of this book and provided very helpful criticism.

Daniela is a big Sergiu Manta fan. Besides her constant support and encouragement to continue my unfortunate biker's story, she also edited the Romanian version of the book – which is no small task.

To Monica Ramirez, great writer and good friend, for advice, support and for 'adopting' me as her sister. Who knows? Maybe one day we'll have your Alina Marinescu and my Sergiu Manta step on each other's toes.

To my family, who support and protect me, so that I can write without any worries.

To Tritonic Publishing and to Bogdan Hrib for trusting my work and promoting it. And to my fellow writers at Tritonic for being a real team.

To Quentin Bates and Marina Sofia, who made this English version possible.

And, of course, to all my readers.